YO-BQT-730

GLADDEN ENTERTAINMENT presents

A MARSHALL BRICKMAN Film

THE MANHATTAN PROJECT

JOHN LITHGOW CHRISTOPHER COLLET CYNTHIA NIXON

Music by PHILIPPE SARDE

Director of Photography BILLY WILLIAMS, B.S.C.

Production Designer PHILIP ROSENBERG

Produced by JENNIFER OGDEN and MARSHALL BRICKMAN

Written by MARSHALL BRICKMAN and THOMAS BAUM

Directed by MARSHALL BRICKMAN

Distributed by TWENTIETH CENTURY FOX FILM CORPORATION

GLADDEN ENTERTAINMENT CORPORATION

AVON
PUBLISHERS OF BARD, CAMELOT, DISCUS AND FLARE BOOKS

THE MANHATTAN PROJECT

by David Bischoff

Based on the screenplay by
Marshall Brickman and Thomas Baum

Grateful acknowledgment is made for permission to reprint a stanza from "The Yew Tree" by Brian McNeil; copyright © 1984 by Egerton Music.

THE MANHATTAN PROJECT is an original publication of Avon Books.
This work has never before appeared in book form.

AVON BOOKS
A division of
The Hearst Corporation
1790 Broadway
New York, New York 10019

Copyright © 1986 by Gladden Entertainment Corporation
Cover Art Copyright © 1986 by Twentieth Century Fox Film Corporation
and Gladden Entertainment Corporation
Published by arrangement with Gladden Entertainment Corporation
Library of Congress Catalog Card Number: 85-91541
ISBN: 0-380-75125-9

First Avon Printing: May 1986

AVON TRADEMARK REG. U.S. PAT. OFF. AND IN OTHER COUNTRIES, MARCA REGISTRADA, HECHO EN U.S.A.

Printed in the U.S.A.

K-R 10 9 8 7 6 5 4 3 2 1

To Ellen Donohue

for the lessons in love
at Ground Zero

THE MANHATTAN PROJECT

Chapter One

National Universities
High Energy Physics Project

A smile spread on Dr. John Mathewson's elfin features as he slotted the key.

Voilà! Lead into gold!

The key turned easily. The procedure had been practiced many times in preparation for this demonstration. No slipup could be chanced here. Not when some of the most important government officials and scientists were watching. Too much was at stake.

The keyhole itself was H-shaped and attached to a flat silvery cone.

Right on beat, like the reaction to the downsweep of a conductor's baton, the machines commenced their music. Lights sprang along the control panel, blazing red and green and blue in circles and squares. This mechanical orchestration started building into its movements: throbbing, humming, pulsing.

Beethoven, thought Mathewson, *eat your heart out! Cyclotron Symphony in D Minor!*

Unable to suppress a wink to an assistant, Mathewson turned to the board where dials indicated voltage and amperage flowing into the equipment in millions of electron volts. *Oh, marvelous MeV's,* the scientist thought. *Do your stuff!*

He hit the start button.

Lights sprang out, flashing across the faces of Drs. Arnold and Swerfinger, old-fogey physicists that they were. Across the faces of Messrs. Henderson and Brown, tight-sphinctered government officials from some top-secret government agency who controlled the purse strings Mathewson needed loosened. This light poured like the rockets' red glare over General Moorhouse, paragon of the Pentagon, and some nameless aide.

DANGER! read a sign nearby. HIGH VOLTAGE! HIGH MAGNETIC FIELD! REMOVE ALL METALLIC OBJECTS FROM YOUR PERSON!

All personnel here were bannered in shiny film badges and green clearance badges.

This was by no means an easy place to get into.

It had taken Mathewson years to make it.

Years.

But he was here now, and it was his shining moment. The tons of machinery, including enormous vacuum pumps worked to capacity, started to shake.

"Christ!" said Henderson, grabbing hold of a chair, eyes darting about fearfully. "What's going on?" He'd already loosed the tie of his gray pin-striped suit. A silver cuff link glittered in the weird light as he reached out to grab something solid.

"Don't worry," said Mathewson, smiling and reassuring them. "This happens all the time, and we haven't blown the thing up yet!"

Uh-oh!

Mathewson's eye caught the quiver of a needle as it edged over into its DANGER-RED area. He leaned over calmly as you please, even as the regular overhead lighting began to pulse with alarm and the whine became higher and higher, to make an adjustment.

A high-voltage spark snapped from his fingertip to the knob.

Mathewson smiled and winked at the others as

he turned the control, the sensation in his arm mar-velous, a foreshadowing *frisson* of what was in store. Now for a little melodrama, he thought mischie-vously...

...and he nudged another button.

Small objects started to fly toward the accelerator.

After all, mused Mathewson, what we have here is one incredibly powerful magnet. A little show, if you will, along with the tell!

Adam Lockhearn, one of his lab assistants, picked up a coffee cup on cue and added a metal spoon. Released, the spoon flew out of the cup and clanged against the domelike wall of the accelerator. Good place to keep it!

A metal pendant around the neck of Marge Rey-nolds, another assistant, jumped up from her chest, standing straight out, horizontal with this invisible force.

Enough, thought Mathewson, satisfied with this little visual illustration of power, satisfied also that power was at sufficiently high level. The coffee and cologne and human smells had now long given way to the ozone scent of pure power. Now for the real show.

He stabbed a forefinger at a button marked LASER INJECT.

Suddenly a laser tube nearby flashed a dazzling green all along its length, accompanied by enormous electrical explosions.

CRACK! it proclaimed in the voice of a Norse god. *CRACK! CRACK!*

One more visual check on his instruments assured John that all machinery was in full alignment; everything was A-okay and *go!* to the max.

Oh frabjous day! he thought as this greenish light bathed the amazed onlookers. How many pieces of chalk have sacrificed themselves on hard blackboard for this moment of glory! How many years he had spent scraping by at the university wasting his time with students while his real work had to be confined to the time crammed between classes! Look at them!

he thought, an odd, devilish smile crossing his features. Only this way can you show dolts the sublime beauties of mathematics and quantum physics theory!

He turned his gaze to a glass cylinder at the other end of the laser tube within a glove box. Any moment...

Yes! Now!

A viscous green fluid started to drip, one drop a second, into this oddly shaped cylinder.

Joe Montgomery, dexterous star assistant of the mad doctor, nimbly took a sample of this delightful stuff and placed it where a reading could be made on the digital-scan particle/emission reader, rather like a sophisticated Geiger counter.

And there it is, Mathewson observed.

The oscilloscope curve! Perfect!

Hard copy was imminent!

Sure enough, the digital readout counter froze the oscilloscope picture and printed it out in hard copy.

And the assay read:

LASER/ISOTOPE SEPARATION
PLUTONIUM ASSAY—SAMPLE #234.AX

ISOTOPE	PERCENTAGE
Pu 239	99.997
Pu 240	00.002
Other	00.001

Mathewson tore this off and passed it around among his captive audience, the vibrations of his machines running through him like a top-quality massage.

He relished this moment terribly. A watershed moment, this. From here he would be in the golden land he had struggled for lo, these long years. Mathematics into solid respect, physics into government grants. Lead into gold!

Government flunky Henderson's eyes grew huge.

"Jesus Christ!" Awe was all over the man. "Ninety-nine point nine nine seven?"

The noise was so great from the machines the man had to yell to make himself heard.

John, however, did not raise his voice at all.

"Purest plutonium in the universe."

He winked at them and gave them his by now trademark smile.

"Pretty, isn't it?"

James Henderson of the Internal Security Division of the Department of Defense of the United States of America dug in his jacket pocket for his pack of Camels.

"Jesus," he said, fumbling one of the little bastards out and lighting it as he walked into the control room of the university research lab. "Jesus, Mary, and Joe."

This was going to put them about twenty goddamn years ahead of the Russians. Why, with something like this little breakthrough, properly used, old man Gorbachev would be on his peasant knees, licking Yankee tail!

As he sucked on the smoke—sucked it deep into his lungs, letting the nicotine add wings to the excitement already speeding through his bloodstream—he recognized the elation he felt and had to smile. He brushed back his thinning brown hair as the memories came. It was like when he played football in college, and the score was a dead tie, the other team looking about unbeatable. And then the quarterback would call the secret plan that the coach had come up with, and the ball was snapped and hundreds of pounds of hard male flesh were pounding the turf and the plastic and the uniform cloth, and suddenly that sweet pigskin was sailing, sailing through the air straight to the receiver, who stood, uncovered, just yards from goal!

Yeah!

Henderson shivered with excitement, and watched while the others of his group—Brown, Dr. Arnold and Dr. Swerfinger, General Moorhouse and Lieutenant Knob—filed into the room. Brown, a heavyset dull-eyed henchman kind of guy, was carrying a tray holding envelopes. He placed it on the table, and the group began reclaiming watches, pocket change, keys, and other personal metal objects from the envelopes.

Henderson saw that the expressions of the others were a reflection of what was churning deep inside of himself. He glanced down to the lab, where Dr. John Mathewson was supervising his amazing equipment.

He turned to the general, who was slipping a government ballpoint pen into his pocket.

"Bob? What do you think?"

The general looked as though he'd caught a few passes in his time, been tackled a few times as well. His eyes were granite-hard.

"A weapon this big"—the general held his hands about eight inches apart—"with twenty times the punch of anything anybody's got?" He turned to the scientists. "Is he kidding? Is that what he's got? I mean, is that what we can do?"

"Precisely," said Swerfinger, and there was something else in the man's expression that Henderson noted. Professional envy. "No. He did just that, all right. It's a brilliant achievement. Brilliant." Spoken with something less than enthusiasm.

"He'd get the Nobel if he could publish," murmured Arnold.

Brown, fastening an expensive Swiss watch around a swarthy wrist, looked up and scowled. "Publish?"

The scientist held up a defensive hand. "I said *if*."

Henderson glanced down again at Dr. Mathewson, thought for a moment.

Yes, that ball was sailing, flying straight on for the receiver. And the goal was within reach.

Now it was his job to make sure that oval bit of victory got tucked safely under the running back's arms and no bad guys had a shot at those speeding legs.

He sat down in his chair, pulled out another Camel, and lit it from the nearly dead cigarette.

He took a puff of fresh tobacco, then stubbed the abandoned cigarette out in an ashtray.

"All right," he said with finality, authority. "I want a prototype facility. Fully operational. Before Geneva if possible."

He turned to Brown.

"Yeah. And everything goes through Energy in Washington, you hear? I want this to seem very far away from Defense, you understand? Need-to-know; cosmic clearance."

Henderson swiveled his chair and peered down at the good doctor in his marvelous laboratory. "He's made some requests that aren't normal. It's not what we usually do, but this time it's worth it. We'll give him what he needs, professionally and...personally."

The other scientists raised their eyebrows and glanced at each other.

"Set him up," continued Henderson. "Whatever he needs. Someplace quiet, away from prying eyes." He blew a cloud of smoke. "And keep an eye on him. This isn't exactly small potatoes."

Brown nodded.

Henderson closed his eyes and balled his fist.

Go, team, go! he thought, feeling the machines throb their power below his feet.

Chapter Two

The explosion produced a huge cloud of smoke, shaped like a mushroom. It reached black and billowing for the sky.

Paul Stephens shook his head in disgust.

"Pathetic," he said as he slouched in the living-room couch, holding the remote controls loosely in one hand. "Asinine!" he yelped at the TV screen.

Mr. Wizard and two cute children emerged from behind a thick oak. Mr. Wizard pointed up to the model rocket ascending to a height somewhat short of the stars. "You can imagine, kids, the *thrill* that Robert Goddard felt when he began his career in rocketry."

"Yeah, sure," Paul Stephens murmured. "He just wanted to blow things up, like all we scientists do!" He grinned and munched on a Dorito, straight from the bag. The lanky blond sixteen-year-old knew that with the stuff in his workshop downstairs alone he could build a *much* better rocket than this jerk yakking away about his pathetic little bangers even a model rocket company like Estes wouldn't palm off as rockets! What a bunch of wimps! Why, this Dorito he was crunching made more sound than this wimp could!

"But you must remember, kids," said a serious Mr. Wizard as he bent a parental frown down to the milk-sucking moppets. "You must never play with explosives without adult supervision. I'm simply illustrating a scientific principle here. Firecrackers and rockets can be just like bombs, and you might"— deep, *deep* frown—"blow somebody up. And that somebody might be you!"

Paul laughed, bits of corn chip spewing on the rug.

"Well, of course you can blow yourself up, turkey!" he said, switching with contempt to MTV. "That's part of the fun."

As he cleaned up his mess on the rug (wouldn't Mom just love *that*) and Sioxie and the Banshees wailed through a video, he decided that yeah, he was in the mood to dabble with the old chemistry set. It was Friday now, and a whole weekend loomed ahead of him, ripe for mischief. He'd just wander on down to the supply store, purchase a few "safe" chemicals, and dabble. Stephens the alchemist! Stephens the master of the elements!

Nothing nasty, mind you. Just some brilliant variation on the old Power Powder ... stuff he could pull neat practical jokes with! Paul Stephens loved practical jokes. He had a few ideas of which ones he'd pull. Yeah. Too bad Richard wasn't here for the fun.

The thought made him close his eyes for a moment. Richard. Good old Richard. Richard Yates sure as hell wasn't going to pull any more practical jokes. Paul Stephens would just have to do Richard's share. It was his duty, he thought sadly.

He tossed the chips on the coffee table morosely and watched as Nina Blackwood bobbed her shaggy head like some dashboard doll, yapping about Madonna's new baby.

"I can't imagine what they're going to call it!" said Paul Stephens to the TV set.

The sound of a closing door brought him to his feet, unable to suppress his anticipation. "Mom!" he called, checking around for stray chip specks. "That you?"

"Of course it's me, silly," said his mother, walking into the living room, arms full. "Who else would it be?"

"Could be that chain-saw killer, Mom!" Gee, she looked nice. He didn't have a dog for a mother, that was sure!

"Well, if he does show up, could you have him take care of that dead tree in the back? Winter's coming on and we need some firewood."

Paul went to her as she set her bag down and gave her an impulsive kiss.

"Well, there goes the mother–son distancing process I learned in psych," she said, returning the favor lightly.

"Don't get too excited. Just my Oedipus complexion."

"Spotty at best," she said. "I got your tapes."

"Great!"

"That's what the kiss was for, wasn't it? Well, I deserve another one, because I stopped at the record store for Ann, and I saw something you might like."

She pulled an LP from one of the bags.

"Mom! The new Shriekback album!" said Paul. He admired it a moment, realizing that he was a pretty lucky guy to have a mom who knew who Shriekback were, let alone nice enough to buy him the new album. . . . Then he got suspicious. "This some kind of bribe?"

"Uh, no, Paul," she said, taking off her coat and hanging it in the closet. "A guilt offering. I'm going out tonight. A guy asked me out."

For a moment, Paul was speechless.

"But, Mom! You were supposed to watch these tapes with me!" he said, unable to hide the disappointment in his voice.

"I know, dear," she said, hauling the groceries into the kitchen. "But when you're my age, you've got to take the dates when you get them. Especially if you're a single mother with a teenage son."

He plopped down in the dining-room chair desolately and pulled out the tape from the video rental store. *Kind Hearts and Coronets*. Just like he'd asked for. But now he didn't have anyone to watch it with! And he'd asked for it especially so his mom could see it.

"I hope he's taking you for champagne and caviar!" Paul called sarcastically.

"Hardly," his mother called back. "Ice hockey game. I bought your favorite kind of frozen pizza, and some extra cheese and pepperoni, and I'm sure that with your extraordinary abilities in chemistry, you'll be able to whip up a gourmet's delight for your gustatory pleasures this evening. Oh, and don't forget we've still got lots of Orville Redenbacker's, and I got some more butter and—"

"Mom! You don't even *like* ice hockey!"

She appeared at the doorway. "Simple principle, dear. You do what they like until they like you so much they don't care."

"Ugh. Whatever happened to women's lib? Sports are disgusting!"

"Builds character, they say," she said, going to him, giving him a gentle hug. "I guess that's why your character is so warped, huh?"

Paul detached himself and moped into the living room. "I just can't believe it! Mom, *Kind Hearts* is a great film." He spun around. "Hey, why don't you ask this dork...I mean, this guy, to stay and watch with us! If he likes the movies, he's got my approval. If he doesn't, you can just kick him out."

She shook her head sadly. "Paul, you clearly just don't understand. There's more to life than video and rock and British stuff and books and your little experiments!"

Paul was honestly baffled. "What?"

"Sex!"

"Mom!"

"Oh, I don't mean the hard stuff, though God knows I get little enough of that....I mean the opposite sex, dear. I need someone.... Since your father and I have split up ... well—"

"Mom, spare me, huh?"

"You'll understand one day, dear."

"Yeah. Sure."

The doorbell rang.

"That must be Joe," she said. "And I haven't changed yet!"

"Joe." Paul tasted the name and found it fairly rancid.

"Be a dear and talk to him ... nicely! ... while I go upstairs and get ready, Paul."

"Sure, Mom." Right. He was always nice to the losers, at least while he checked them out.

"Paul," she said, fixing him with a serious eye. "He's not your dad by a long shot, I know. But he's someone."

The doorbell rang insistently and she went to answer it.

Dad. Good old Dad, happily divorced now and having a high old time in Saudi Arabia.

When his mom came back, a big, dark-haired guy followed her, looking Irish and horny. Sheesh, Mom could sure pick 'em sometimes!

"Paul, this is Joe O'Conner."

The man pushed a beer belly forward and held out a meaty hand for a manly shake. Cripes, the guy had chest hair sticking out of his undershirt! As Paul pumped the hand, he got a snootful of Brut cologne. He felt like puking, but instead managed a quiet "Hihowareyou."

"Nice to meet you, Paul," said Joe, grinning. "Nice-lookin' kid you got here, Liz."

"I would have preferred the plaid variety, but I suppose I made the right choice," said Mom. "Yes. You two have a nice talk while I go and change."

"Don't be too long, now," said Joe Ice-Hockey-Jerk. "Game starts at seven-thirty."

"Yes. Make yourself comfortable, Joe. Paul, tell Joe about your science projects. Joe's a construction manager who works a lot with explosives on his job.

He's a safety expert!" She gave him a meaningful eye, and then was off up the stairs and into her usual dressing frenzy.

Joe settled down. "Got a beer, kid?"

"Sure." Paul was happy to do something besides talk to the guy, so he walked into the kitchen and pulled a John Courage out of the fridge. Mom was cool, and let him have a beer once in a while, as long as he promised not to go out drinking by himself. It was a fair deal, Paul figured, since he got good Brit beer in the bargain and it kept him out of that great teen plague, boozy car accidents.

"What is this?" asked Joe when handed the beer.

"It's from England."

Joe tried it. "No Bud, huh?"

Paul shook his head.

Joe shrugged, and there was a moment of uncomfortable silence.

"Hey, what do you think of the Rams this year?" Joe asked in the way of lame conversational gambits.

"I think they suck."

"What are you talking about? They blew out the Lions on Sunday!"

"I don't care for nonparticipatory sports much, I'm afraid," Paul said, putting it mildly. "Sorry!" He smiled, remembering what his mother had requested: niceness.

"What?" Joe shook his head, seemingly unable to comprehend this un-American, unmanly spectacle of a boy not into sports. "Why, that's...uh...well, I suppose it takes all types, then." He took a swig of his beer. "Uh...interesting stuff."

"Imported," Paul said.

"Yeah. So your Mom says you're a real science whiz. Prizewinner at science fairs for the past five years.... What were the projects?"

Paul rattled off the project titles.

Joe O'Conner blinked. "God. That's quite a mouthful."

"And Mom says you use explosives?"

"That's right. Gotta blow things up sometimes, but you gotta be safe about it."

For the first time, Paul smiled at him glowingly. "Sounds like fun."

Joe, clearly somewhat taken aback by this, changed the subject. "So, you got a date tonight, I guess."

"I had one, but she's going to the ice hockey game."

"Oh. Right. Sorry, kid. But I figure, a nice-lookin' guy like you ... you should be out sowing the old wild ones!"

Joe gave him a nudge-nudge wink-wink smile.

"Yeah. I guess I just don't rate with a lot of the girls at school. Things are pretty weird on the educational front these days."

"Ain't they always?" Joe looked thoughtful and drank some more of the beer, as though thinking, Should I tell him or shouldn't I?

"Listen, Paul. Maybe a few words from a guy who's had some knocks himself might help you out."

Gee, the guy was starting to act human! Paul was impressed. Maybe he'd be okay after all! He could, admittedly, use any help he could get with girls. Thing was, he liked them fine, but most of them seemed in another universe. They looked at him, lacking high-style dress and social caste, as though he were some alien newly arrived on the Starship Special.

"Okay," he said.

"Paul, pal, the women ..." The swarthy brow knitted in deep thought. "Look at it this way. It's like in football. You just gotta get in there and fight! Sure, you get knocked down sometimes, and you don't always score. But if you train proper and you're ready for a scrap ... well, you might get dirty, but soon enough you're gonna have some other jerk's brains on your cleats, and a cheerleader's big tits stickin' in your face!"

Joe smiled with self-satisfaction at this bit of profound masculine philosophy.

Paul Stephens could not speak.

"You've got to be kidding me."

"It's that simple, man!"

"Whew! Darwin was wrong. The human race has devolved!"

"Huh?"

"How's your beer?"

"Kinda sweet and thick for me, pal. I hear those guys in England drink it warm."

"Room temperature."

"Yeah."

Another uncomfortable silence, finally broken by the arrival of his mother, dressed comfortably and attractively in designer jeans and a frilly top and carrying a stylish blue coat.

"Well, I'm ready for battle, Joe," she said. "What have you two gentlemen been talking about?"

"You certainly look nice, Elizabeth," said the heavyset man, rising from the couch. "Paul and I . . . I just asked why he wasn't out with a beautiful lady tonight, like I am!"

"Joe, don't—"

"I'm real sorry to steal your mom away like this, pal. Maybe you can call up a friend."

His mother looked pained. "Joe—"

"It would be long distance," said Paul, standing up and going to the video library above the tape player.

"Got a best friend outta town, huh?"

"You could say that," said Paul, selecting a tape and slipping it into the VCR. "He shot himself in the head three weeks ago."

There was a deadly silence as Paul rewound the tape.

"God! Sorry, pal!" said Joe. "I really didn't know, Elizabeth."

"Paul, you enjoy your movies," said his mom. "C'mon, Joe. We don't want to be late for your game."

"You have a good one, pal," said Joe, his tone pure conciliation.

"Right," said Paul.

The door slammed.

Paul turned the on button, walked back to the couch, picked up the package of Doritos, and began to watch his favorite *Young Ones* episode.

He felt like watching Vivian the Punk play his very favorite game, Murder in the Dark.

Chapter Three

He was dreaming about a field in England.

Above rolling hills, bordered with disciplined hedges of trees, hung an almost-full moon, over which passed shreds of clouds like floating specters. He smelled fresh pasture, and felt the cool of autumn, and through the air, like mist, passed the strains of an old English hymn sung by Steeleye Span, "Harvest Home":

> *Come ye thankful people come,*
> *Raise the sound of Harvest Home.*

And he was nearly leveled by the breathless beauty, the medieval *rightness* of it all.

Of course, it being a much too happy dream, he immediately woke up.

He had the familiar where-the-hell-am-I sensation. Darkness all about, bedclothes and curtain darkness, with the air smelling of stale Coke and Doritos. Blinking, Paul turned to the digital readout clock on his bedtable.

3:30, declared the green numerals.

Groggily Paul reached over and turned on the light.

Damn Richard. Another folky dream. What was a rocker doing dreaming about folk?

He looked around the mess that was his room. *Playboy* magazines were mixed in equal measures with *Omni*s and *Scientific American*s.

Something was wrong. He could feel it in the air.

He could see light seeping under the bedroom door; the hall light was still on. Was his mother home yet?

Of course she was. Mom would maybe give that jerk one date, tops, and that would be a bloody short one!

Still, he'd better check anyway.

He got up, put his robe on over his PJs, and padded out to the hallway. Sixteen years old, and the man of the house! Sheesh, he supposed that if that was the way it was, so be it. Watch out after the lady who changed your diapers and wiped your nose for years ... well, if Dad wouldn't, he supposed he'd have to.

It would be nice, he supposed, if the old man would give a ring once in a while. He'd left, Dad had, more than four years ago, with immaculate timing. Paul could remember mornings, getting up for breakfast with Mom, alone, when things were so miserable that the first thing he did when he got to Clark Junior High was to head for the boys' room and toss his cookies. You could only take so much of that kind of life, when your pop skips and your mom looks like she's about to slash her wrists, before you either lose your mind, or you get strong. Paul had taken the latter course. He'd slowly assumed a lot of the roles of man of the house that his father had once had....

Yeah, he thought as he headed for Mom's bedroom. That was probably why he was worried about dear old Mum. "The child is father to the woman..." Hmm ...something like that. Wordsworth. From English. Good guy.

Of course, he was going to have to make this little trip look totally accidental...a voyage to the bathroom for nocturnal relief. Casually he trudged in his usual half-awake gait down the hall, past the master bedroom.

Which was open. Light on.

Whew!

A few steps past, a faked double take, a few steps back.

His mom was propped up in a mountain of pillows, glasses on, backlit by a reading light, a thick paperback in her hand.

"Oh!" said Paul, giving a smooth little wave. "Hi."

She gazed over at him, then took a glance at her alarm clock on her bed table.

"Paul. It's three-thirty." But she gave him a look that said, But thank God you're here!

Paul stepped in, hands in bathrobe pockets. The room smelled nice...perfume, powder, fresh linen. Nice female smells. Much purer, much nicer, than when the old man smoked his cigars in here.

"What's the book?"

She held it up. On the cover, a naked couple, splashed by an ocean breaker, embraced. The title was *The Selkie.*

His mom didn't look real happy.

"Oh," said Paul, feeling awkward. "Hey. How about I buy you a drink?"

"Sure, sailor. Come round here much?" she said, getting up and putting on a frilly pink dressing gown.

"Yeah, babe. The dames here are the best."

She took his arm, and they walked down the stairs together to the kitchen.

Paul set her up regally on a stool and kissed her hand. *"Enchanté, madame,"* he said.

"Goodness, your pronunciation is getting better."

"Merci. And, *madame,* do you take two one or two lumps of *merde* in your tea?"

She laughed. "But your vocabulary is awful."

"Madame! S'il vous plaît!"

"Anyway, I'd like some cocoa, please."

"Coming up." He went to a cabinet, got out the appropriate stuff. "Formula Three or Formula Four?"

"Heavy on the chocolate, please. Like, how about melting a Hershey bar in the cup too?"

"Le chocolat!" declared Paul in an outrageously

awful accent. "Thees ees the sweet of unrequited loooooove, *oui?*"

"Oh no," she said, a chuckle in her voice. "I thought you were the chemistry expert! It's the drug for frustration."

"Ah," he said, turning away and dealing with the materials. He went to the icebox, poured out some milk in a pan. He set it on the stove, turned up the heat, and looked over at her. "Mr. Ice Hockey wouldn't put out, huh?"

"Paul!"

"You have a good time?" he said with just the right dose of irony in his voice.

"I think you can tell the answer to that already, you dolt! It was awful! I just hope this doesn't screw up things between his company and ours. I should have just politely declined his invitation."

"So you're not going to go out with him again?"

"I don't think he's going to ask!"

"Ah." Paul measured some cocoa powder precisely, scientifically, into a cup marked ELIZABETH, complete with flowers entwined around the letters. "Don't worry, Mom. Somewhere your prince is waiting, but like the song do say, you gotta kiss your share of amphibians first!"

"My share! I've already done about two ponds' worth!" She shook her head and laughed. "But hey, Mr. Pubescent. How's it going on the school front with the young ladies?"

"Don't ask."

"Hey, you get to hear about my love life ... or lack of one, rather. I get to hear about yours!"

Paul watched for bubbles on the side of the metal pan. "Cripes, Mom. The girls these days ... They look like they spend about an hour in the morning in front of the makeup mirror! They look like adults, for godsake, not teenagers, and they can't figure out why guys don't know what to do! About the only guys that get on with the girls at school are the ones that don't really care, they're too busy playing sports or running the school government or acting in stupid plays!"

"You think it's ever been any different, Paul?"

Steam was rising up from the pan. Paul poured, stirred.

"Come on in sometime and look what Ronald Reagan, Calvin Klein, and Max Factor hath wrought!"

"Hmm. Maybe I will."

He brought her the cup of cocoa.

"Watch out," he said. "It's hot."

But she wasn't looking at the cup, she was looking at him. And her blue-green eyes ... they were filling with almost unbearable emotion.

"What?" he said lamely.

She smiled, shook her head, looked over his shoulder, then reached out and smoothed back his hair.

"You're growing so fast."

"Yeah, but it's no reason to have a nervous breakdown!" he said, jittery. Hard to take this much emotion from old Mom. Heavy stuff.

"Come here."

Oh-oh.

She held him in a tight embrace.

He paused for a moment, then returned it gently. And he felt her shudder.

God, what was going on inside the poor woman?

"God. We got to get you a Valium or some heroin or something!"

"No. This will do." She moved away, and blew on her cocoa. "None for you, Paul?" she said shyly.

"Uh-uh. Stunts my growth."

"Oh, I forgot to tell you. Mrs. Yates called. She wants to know when you can come over and pick up that stuff of Richard's she wants you to have."

"You mean, the stuff she wants out of her house beautiful!"

"Paul!" She shot him an angry, motherly look. "You think you're the only one who's upset about Richard? Have some respect for the Yateses' grief!"

"Yeah. Yeah," he said, sighing. "I'm sorry, Mom. I guess it's not their fault they're such shitheads."

"You can't blame anybody, Paul. It just doesn't work." Her eyes turned thoughtful. "You don't blame yourself still, do you, Paul?"

"Maybe I should have some of that stuff, after all," he said, going for some cocoa.

He got himself a cup and poured and looked at the steam coming up, like an escaping spirit.

"Mom," he murmured. "He gave all the signs. If I had listened to him, I might have saved him."

"For how long? A month, a year? He had a deep psychological problem, Paul. Deep inside, there was something wrong with the kid!"

Paul closed his eyes and shook his head. "Uh-uh, Mom. Deep inside, there's something wrong with this culture."

He decided to try and overdose on cocoa.

Chapter Four

It was a beautiful day in Ithaca, New York, but Dr. John Mathewson barely noticed it.

He walked down the main commercial area, through the late-September breeze, and although the walk afforded a brief glimpse of the ice-blue lake, reflecting the surrounding green-and-brown hills, he was contemplating other, more cerebral matters.

He'd been in town two weeks now, staying at the Carriage House Hotel down the road, but mostly staying at MedAtomics, setting up his lab. The work was going well. Production would begin tomorrow. The overseers were very pleased. In fact, this very morning, they had given Mathewson a small packet containing the first installment of his ... additional consideration.

So he'd taken this afternoon off to saunter down the Ithaca avenues and savor the weight and heft and idea of the green stuff riding in the breast pocket of his blazer.

Somewhere in the distance, a jackhammer worked away at pavement. Cars performed their traditional stoplight parades through the town. There was the smell of Chinese food drifting in the air outside the

Jade Mandarin restaurant, but Mathewson was not at all hungry, having wolfed down a quick hamburger at work before leaving. Hamburger with milk, his usual business lunch. Quick and efficient, and he could often do it right in the midst of whatever aspect of the project he was hard at work on.

He stopped at his bank first, where he deposited much of what had been in the envelope. He was amused at the shock of the teller at so much cash. He could have requested a check, he supposed, but this was so much more satisfying.

Mathewson retained enough cash to get what he wanted down the road. He'd seen it the first weekend he was here, and he doubted that it would be gone so soon. So he collected his deposit slip from the pert red-haired lady behind the bank desk, strode out into the delicious day, and headed for the car dealer.

Money had not always been important to Mathewson.

In fact, that perhaps was why he wanted it now. He'd built up absolutely no savings to speak of, and he'd lived in apartments or dormitories all his life, building up no equity in property. On paper he'd been a pauper, his salaries from colleges and the places he'd worked at just enough to live a bohemian lifestyle and funnel the rest into private research. No, for twenty years, ever since he'd gotten into a real lab, that second year at MIT, Mathewson could only sleep, eat, and think practical physics. He'd dated his share of students and co-workers, establishing an easy social and sexual camaraderie with females, but he seldom got very close to any ... and when he did, the ladies involved found themselves playing second fiddle to his machines and computations.

One lady, upon leaving him, had come up with the very best zinger he'd heard: "You don't use baseball scores in bed, John! You analyze the chemical properties of quarks!"

How charming, thought the physicist, laughing to himself.

But then John Mathewson, happy with his work,

had suddenly woken up, destitute, in the eighties. Suddenly women didn't seem to care whether he was brilliant.... He had a harder time finding the rare companion he needed upon emerging from the rarefied atmosphere of research. Why? Because he didn't wear nice clothes. People had forgotten the sixties. Now they wanted to see Quality, they wanted to see Money.... And women ... women wanted Money, sure, and they wanted Security ... not a few rolls in the hay with a brilliant and quirky scientist.

Okay. So be it....

But when he realized that his fellow scientists were getting that way as well ...

Of course, the scientific community had always been about as friendly as bargain night at the cockfights, and one's doctorate was generally merely a ticket to jump in the ring and start slashing away at the dear colleagues. The DNA business with Watson and Crick was the perfect example. But he'd taken it all before as rather a lark, a challenge, a game....

Now, though, when he showed up in his ancient Volkswagen, in a ratty corduroy jacket and with a bottle of cheap Spanish wine, he was not merely looked at askance, but people started laughing up their sleeves at him. That Mathewson, they must be saying. He must really be doing poorly in his research! What a joke! Pass the caviar, dear. Oh, and have you seen Dr. Williams's new Lamberghini?

God! In that kind of atmosphere, what would happen to poor frazzled Einstein?

He could just imagine a college hallway discussion. "Hey, Albert! Did you hear? My new book *Scientific Secrets of the Universe* just made number two on the *New York Times* best-seller list. I've just sold it to the movies, and Burt Reynolds and Dolly Parton are going to star. Really, Al, you ought to watch those crumbs in the sweater ... lice food. Mine? ... oh, the best cashmere. Goes well with the silk tie, don't you think? Don't touch, you've got chalk all over your fingers! Ugh!"

So now, though he could not publish his break-through, John Mathewson intended to show off in different ways. He'd show those simpletons at MIT this year at homecoming. Oh yes, he'd show them!

He could just imagine all the invitations he'd get from ladies to visit their condos!

But he had to do it all with the Mathewson flair, the Mathewson dash, and somehow, this next bit was just the right underline to the clothes he would buy, the wine he would bring, the Brie he would delicately consume!

Mathewson crossed the next lane with the WALK light and headed through the huge glass doors below a sign that said ITHACA MERCEDES-BENZ.

It almost seemed as though the saleman were lying in wait for him.

"Ah... Mr. Masterson!" said the thin, balding little guy, eyes bugging just a bit.

"That's Mathewson. Hello." Hands shook.

"I don't know how much longer we're going to be able to keep this work of art here," said the salesman, a man by the name of Jesse Richards. "There's been a lot of interest from various highly placed Cornell professors."

"Ah, I see. Mind if I look again?"

It was a vintage-model Mercedes, gray, finely crafted, with all the amenities... and certainly not diesel-fueled!

"Did I mention, Mr. Mathews, that we've had the finest imported leather worked into the interior? A Fisher stereo, with both tape player and CD player. Only the finest quality."

Mathewson looked at it, pursed his lips.

"I'll take it," he said.

The salesman blinked.

"Ah. Excellent. I think we can arrange it... the price..."

"The price will be fine."

"If you'll come this way, then, sir!"

The salesman led Mathewson to a desk and took out various items of paperwork.

"Now, then, before I start filling this out, you must understand that I'll need to know what method of financing you'll be using. We'll need credit references, and certainly at least a 20 percent down payment... I realize that's high, but we must take the proper measures at an establishment of our reputation...."

"Financing," said Mathewson. "Yes, I'll take care of that right now."

He took out the envelope, slipped out four ten-thousand-dollar bills, and placed them, fanned, upon the desk.

"Ah..." said the salesman, stunned for only a second, then breaking out into a huge smile. "Welcome to Ithaca, Mr. Mathewson!"

Chapter Five

Paul Stephens was in his elements.

Flask in hand, he poured a liquid into the red crystals at the bottom. A quick stir from a glass rod, and *voilà!* Black gook!

"Weird," said Tennis Allbow, leaning close to inspect this novel substance, his angular spotty face reflecting in the glass, distortion of a distortion.

Max Perkins looked up and across the science lab of Ithaca High School, where clusters of students huddled around their lab tables, like asylum inmates imitating scientists. Their tables were hopelessly cluttered with flasks and beakers and tubings, right beside purses and Walkmans and teenage-romance paperbacks. Their concoctions as usual, as Paul so often observed, were one part chemical, one part monkey business, and one part pure gossip.

"He's coming!" said Max, pointing excitedly at the distant doorway from the hall. "Hurry up, Paul! The asshole is coming!"

Emma Wilkins was just arriving as well. Her ears perked up at the word *asshole*. "What are you guys going to do to Roland?" she said, her green eyes sparkling amidst her angel-blond hair.

Paul ignored her. He was too excited. This stuff was going to work, he knew it! Now all he had to do was to show off his chemical prowess to his fellow students in typical teenage fashion. This age did indeed have its moments!

"Watch!" he said, moving over to Roland's work area furtively, unable to keep the tremble of excitement from his voice. He grabbed a long eyedropper from a rack, sucked up some of this Wonder Gunk from the bottom of the flask. Then, carefully, he filled the keyhole of the second drawer of Roland Worster's desk.

Finished, he glanced up and around, to make sure the wrong eyes had not witnessed this mischief.

"What is that stuff?" Tennis asked, scratching back his reddish wiry hair as he peered down at Roland's desk.

Max grinned as he noted that Roland had stopped a moment to examine some bit of paper on the bulletin board. "Shh!" he said. "Nitrogen trioxide."

"Yeah," said Tennis, stuttering a bit with excitement. "B-b-but what does it do?"

"It's highly unstable with respect to shock," Max answered, scrunching around on his stool, eyes shiny.

"What's that mean?" Tennis wanted to know.

"You'll see," returned Max, nervously adjusting his suspenders. "Once it dries, if you touch it, it explodes!"

Pretty eyelashes batted as their owner gazed over at the effector of this little prank. "Paul," said Emma. "You're crazy!"

Paul returned to his own stool, taking his place calmly, and with great aplomb and grace, he thought, for a gawky teenager. "You say that like it's a bad thing."

Craig Martin, the group's jock, had just arrived, catching only the tail end of this little dialogue. He slipped his books into their place, adjusted his lettered sweater self-confidently, and bent a toothy smile toward his classmates. "So, then, comrades. Whose desk?"

"Roland Worster's," said Terry Marshall, observing intently from her perch at another table. "I think I'm going to enjoy this!"

Emma shook her head. "Poor Roland. He really should treat the class pranksters more kindly."

"Oh, don't worry," said Paul, washing out the eyedropper in the sink, then slipping it into his desk. He could always use a spare eyedropper. "Nah, he'll love it. Builds character."

Tittering, the kids resumed their serious and constructive student attitudes as the class filled in with the remainder of its complement.

Roland Worster lumbered their way, humongous briefcase thumping on thick thigh, eyes bulging behind their thick eyeglass lenses. Without so much as a good-morning to his classmates, he dropped his case on the desk and started unloading books into their drawers.

Oh boy, oh boy!

"Hey, Roland," said Paul, watching with fascination as the paunchy fellow unloaded his books. "Could I borrow your English notes?" Roland was an ace at English, and he took the very best, most comprehensive notes imaginable.

Roland stuck his lumpy nose up in the air and said, as stuffily as some English lord might, "You've *got* to be kidding, Stephens."

"But I lent you my math homework about ten times!" He looked at the other students as though to say, You see, guys, justice shall be done this day!

"Sorry, Stephens. It's a dog-eat-dog world out there. I gotta look out for number one."

Right. Dog eat dog, thought Paul. Straight from Bullshit 101 from the College of Hard Knocks.

Thing about Roland Worster wasn't that he was a total jerk, with his dorky manner and his horror-movie ugliness.... It was just that he didn't have the grace to be even faintly aware of his totally pathetic state. Even toads were neat if they smiled and tried to be friendly and helpful. But Worster! Worster fancied himself Winston Churchill or something, without any of Churchill's wit or charm. He was the kind of guy that Paul despised the most...the sort who bought Ye Olde Domination crap whole hog, who didn't even *think* about the social and moral implications. This guy was already planning to be a top executive at some power-mad corporation or something...

Yeeeuchh!

Savoring the wonderful smells of mixing chemicals and Emma's Opium perfume, Paul watched eagerly as Roland Worster opened a drawer—the wrong one—stuffed in *Norton's English Literature Anthology,* and closed it briskly.

The teenagers furtively watching all this started as the bell rang with its usual abrupt clamor.

Beginning of class!

Behold, the lecture begins, thought Paul, opening his notebook to take down the pearls of wisdom dropping from the mouth of Mr. Emmitt Wilke.

The teacher performed his usual preamble, talking about this or that of no consequence, skinny hands whipping about occasionally above his long-nosed face with a kind of halfhearted I-have-to-say-this-four-more-times-today excitement.

Yeah, but, Mr. Wilke, thought Paul, you and your Wilke ilk don't bother to tell these poor bemused hormone-pumped people you call students what all this deliciously aesthetic gobbledygook means in their lives! They can't relate, and no wonder. They don't see the practical uses—except maybe, these days, making money—of math and science.

Paul knew, though. No one had taught him how make nitrogen trioxide. He'd learned it himself.

And look at *its* practical purpose!

Paul chuckled to himself.

Any time now old Roland was going to open and close that drawer.

What delicious suspense!

Wilke, meantime, had just completed his drawings of plutonium 239 and 240 on the blackboard, hardly works of art, Paul observed, but accurate enough.

"Last time," the teacher said in his nasal voice, "we learned that plutonium is perfectly suited for the release of enormous amounts of energy due to its ability to fission under the action of slow neutrons. Now, here we have the isotope Pu 239 and here"—tap, tap—"here we have Pu 240." He went to a table and held up two drawings. "And here we have two interesting inventions based on this principle."

Meantime, Paul was ignoring all this. He knew it all anyway; had read it long ago. Simple shit. What was more interesting now, *far* more interesting, was the sight of Roland Worster, fidgeting at his desk, compulsively taking notes, placing and replacing his mountain of books, opening and closing several of the workbench/desk's drawers... but (O perversity, here is thy sting!) never going near the special one, the one rigged with the tiny bit of explosive.

Paul glanced nervously at the others, who seemed equally upset by this delicious but unbearable anticipation. Together, they watched rotund Roland's every move.

Wilke thumped the boards holding the two schematic drawings. One pictured a gun-type fission bomb. The other illustrated an implosion bomb. Paul vaguely noted this, but still paid little attention. Of course they were properly labeled—Wilke was meticulous at that sort of thing—and below the names, they carried additional legends. The former said HIROSHIMA BOMB. The latter read NAGASAKI BOMB. The general heading for them both was NUCLEAR FAST-FISSION DEVICES.

"Can anyone tell us the principle behind the implosion device?" asked Wee Willie Wilke.

Cripes! The sucker was doing it!

Roland opened the second drawer of his desk!

The explosive one!

The girl sitting just to the other side him was Jenny Anderman, whom Paul considered the prettiest and classiest lady in the whole motley class. She was wearing a tight blue sweater, and her blond hair was just perfect now ... and she seemed to sense something was amiss, because she turned that pretty face toward Paul, and their gazes locked...

And Paul just lost himself for a moment in their blue-green beauty.

"Paul," said the teacher. "Paul, could you enlighten us?"

Paul did not respond.

"Mr. Stephens, please tell us the answer!" Wilke said insistently.

"Huh?"

"Stephens, this is the fourth time this—"

And suddenly Paul's skin was saved by the opening of the door, and the entrance of the balding and bespectacled Dr. Avery and several foreign-looking types. Mostly Oriental, probably Japanese.

That's right, thought Paul. He'd heard that there would be several foreign educators roaming the halls today, checking into the wonderful and woolly mysteries of the American educational system.

Dr. Avery gave the teacher a professionally friendly nod and said, "Don't mind us, Mr. Wilke. Carry on!"

Japs! thought Paul, most amused. Yeah, and here was old Wilke going on about the kinds of bombs that had sent thousands and thousands of the poor Japanese to Buddhist nirvana. Paul hoped the fascist had the grace to be embarrassed.

But nooooo! Wilke seemed to be actually pleased to show off.

"Thank you, Dr. Avery."

The other kids ... Max and Tennis and Emma ... were all looking at each other with terror and Oh-shit! expressions.

They all looked at Paul, who just sighed and shrugged fatalistically.

A karmic catastrophe, without question.

"Right," said Mr. Wilke, losing his place slightly in the flow of things. "The implosion technique."

Good old brown-noser Roland seized his opportunity by the throat. He thrust his hand up and waved it excitedly, trying to win brownie points with both Wilke and Avery. Gosh, what a golden opportunity for the dickhead!

Wilke, pleased at class participation, smiled at this sterling student. "Yes, Roland."

Roland stood up, with a pitying, superior look at Paul.

Paul smiled back.

Roland rattled off the answer as he hatefully looked at Paul.

"Yes, your implosion design simply uses a chemical high explosive of weapons-grade plutonium 239 until it's supercritical, thereby producing an atomic explosion."

"Thank you, Roland," said Mr. Roland.

"Thank *you,* Mr. Wilke."

And Roland sat down with a self-satisfied smirk on his fat kisser and, with a triumphant flourish, shut the second drawer of his desk.

BANG! came the explosion.

FLASH! came the bright splatter of light.

WHOOSH! went the fat plume of smoke, drifting up toward the ceiling, black and stinky.

A moment of astonished silence held all the class and the visitors and the teachers in thrall.

Then applause began, along with cheers.

The Japanese joined in, perhaps believing this to be some cheerful American display of their explosive might. Good show, and how typically silly of them!

But then, with Mr. Avery's and Mr. Wilke's expressions turning quite red, they stopped, confused, and plastered bemused smiles on their faces.

Paul shook his head, gave a David Letterman look of terrible chagrin, and caught a disapproving look from Jenny, a boys-will-be-boys look.

But there was something more behind it…she seemed to be secretly *enjoying* this.…

An interesting person, definitely!

For his part, Roland was doing a fair share of

blustering and flustering, standing back up, looking as though he were about to undergo a heart attack.

Shaking with fury, the big student stabbed an accusing finger at Paul. "He did this!" he cried, comically red-faced. "Him! Him! Paul Stephens! He's sick!"

Oh, without a doubt, thought Paul Stephens as he looked over at the nonplussed foreign visitors and Dr. Avery, who was giving him his patented pissed-off-pedagogue glare.

He was sick of all these jerks!

Chapter Six

The bell rang.

With clattering, clunking, and chattering, the students rapidly departed the science lab as Mr. Wilke watched, face still holding a bit of angry pink.

"Stephens, I trust you'll do me the favor of lingering for a moment," he commanded sarcastically.

"I've already got an appointment later today with Mr. Avery. Won't that do?"

"No," said Wilke, heading over to a particularly messy desk, examining the scattered test tubes, beakers, and tubing with distaste. "No, he'll only torture you for his own satisfaction. I merely wish to talk."

"Iron maiden?"

"No, that's his wife. It'll be the rack, I think, Stephens. Creak, creak, squeak. Exquisite pain. You do have fun, you hear? He's recording it all for the weekly teachers' meeting. I'll think we'll all get a yock out of it."

Paul chuckled, watching as Mr. Wilke set to the task of clearing up this clutter so that his next class, already beginning to filter in, could decimate it again.

"You've got to admit, Mr. Wilke, Roland Worster deserved it! I am merely an instrument of the gods!"

Wile speared him with a nasty glare. "Thor's jockstrap, huh?"

"Really, Mr. Wilke. Surely sometime in your life you've been a robust, fun-loving, prank-pulling kid!"

"This is neither the time...nor the place, Stephens. This is not a fun-loving age. We are dealing with a very serious problem here....Do you know how hard it is to keep order in a class without this kind of thing?"

"Ah yes...this age of wonders," said Paul, taking his turn at sarcasm. "We pierce the skies, and Reagan wants to use the satellites to burn holes in things." He picked up some tubing and zapped an imaginary Russian.

"Somehow, somewhere, you've lost your sense of priorities, Stephens. Here at Ithaca High, we pride ourselves at having one of the best systems of education in the country. But not for merely the sake of education, or for the clearly superior intellects of our students...." He paused and straightened his glasses. "We also prepare our students for the realities that will face them when they head for college...and the professional world. This is a very competitive age, Stephens. It is our duty, as teachers, to make sure that our charges are fully equipped with the necessary weapons of knowledge to grapple with the fight that awaits them."

"Fight? Fight for what?"

"Why, professional status, further knowledge, success...why, personal and social progress, man!" Wilke looked at Paul as though he were an alien. "Everything that Western civilization stands for...grounded, of course, in the nuclear family."

Paul leaned over a sink and started making loud vomiting noises.

"What are you doing?" said Wilke, losing his cool.

"Whew," said Paul, wiping imaginary spittle from his mouth. "I've been swallowing that kind of shit for so long, I just automatically do a Technicolor yawn whenever I hear it in such pure form."

Seeing more students drift in, Wilke renewed his attempts at getting the place in order. "There really isn't any more room in this society for that kind of rebellious attitude. And good riddance to it! I think, frankly, that the Reagan era, and the new priorities among young people, will prove sociologically to be a breakthrough in American history."

"You mean the yuppies are gonna rewrite everything...in a ledger book, probably. And hey, Mr. Wilkes, how much money do *you* make? Not much, huh?"

Wilke tried to close a drawer, but it was stuck.

"Damn it, Stephens. What are you trying to prove, anyway?" Push, push. "You keep it up, Avery's really going to chop your head off! You won't graduate, you won't get into college..." Grunt. "I mean, damn it, man, it's such a waste. You could be the brightest kid in the class. You *are* the brightest kid in the class. I mean, I think you are. I don't know anymore. You're pissing it all away. Why?"

Paul leaned over, gave the drawer a slight tug, and it slipped in easily.

"I guess I'm just self-destructive, sir." He smiled, grabbed his books, and made for his next class.

Lunchtime.

Well, thought Paul, walking his bike, idly ignoring the lustrous day and the stunning scenery arrayed about Ithaca, a beautiful ring on the tip of a Finger Lake. Well, at least a progressive school doesn't force you to stay in at lunch hour and chow down on Mystery Meat.

He could just tool on down atop his classy Sears ten-speed to Marino's, chew on a steak-and-cheese Philly style, and see what trouble good old Tad Martin was getting into today on *All My Children.* Was he going to finally get into Hillary's pants, or what?

He hoisted himself atop the bike and let it roll

gently downward through the parking lot...and then he braked for a moment.

Some distance away, he spotted Jenny, standing next to her car, talking to a nice-looking blond guy holding a Frisbee. The guy then tossed the Frisbee to a guy running along a grassy stretch, then ran off himself to receive the next pass.

Fun, fun, fun! thought Paul.

He rolled down, watching Jenny, thinking, That's the thing about girls pretty as her. They make you think there are ideals like truth and beauty and stuff like that.

God, she was cute!

Jenny seemed to be looking for something in a black pocketbook. If that thing was anything like his mom's, then she wasn't going to find it, that was for sure.

Here's your chance, hotshot, he thought.

"Lose something?" he asked her.

She looked up and smiled absently. "Oh. Hi, Paul. It's so dumb. I locked my car keys in the glove compartment 'cause I always lose them. So *now* I seem to have lost the key to the glove compartment, right? Forget it...."

Paul parked his bike, got off.

"You got a nail file in there?"

"A girl without a nail file? Yeah, sure. Why?"

"Could I see it?"

Jenny fished out a nail clipper and handed it to him, curiosity open on her well-defined features.

"You're gonna pick the lock?"

"Uh-huh." He got in the car and examined the box. Yep. A lot like his mom's, and he'd fooled around with that, and every other lock within reach. Yeah. If he did get tossed out of school, he could always become a burglar or something.

"That was terrible, you know."

Paul commenced fiddling, sticking in the file, jiggling.

"What you did to Roland."

"Terrible?" he said. "I thought it was very effective."

There, just the right twist, and the lock opened.

The lid opened like a surprised mouth gasping.

"Hey. Not bad. Thanks!" Toss of lustrous locks. "Where'd you learn that?"

Paul blew on his fingers, then rubbed them against his chest with a self-satisfied smile. "CIA. Child recruitment program!"

Jenny shook her head, sending off a whiff of delightful perfume. She got in the car, shut the door, stuck the key in the ignition, then paused for a moment, as though considering something.

"Listen..." she said, turning back to him. "What are you doing Sunday night?"

"Nothing. Why?"

"This lab test coming up...I'm a little stumped on some of the equations. You want to study?"

"Together?" Paul asked, trying all he was worth not to do something stupid like gulp.

"Uh-huh."

Paul blinked and gazed after the guy who had just left, the blond god. "What about Mr. Perfect?"

"Who, Eric? Don't worry about Eric. He's just pretty."

Bam!

Suddenly a Frisbee whammoed into the back of his head.

Absently he picked it up. He'd already been kicked in the head by something far stronger...infatuation!

Casually he hefted it in his hand.

"Paul!" said Jenny, a tiny pout in her voice. "You're not concentrating!"

"No. Sure! Right!" He grinned cockily down at her. "Study! Where?"

"My house, okay? It's 115 North Highland, near Woodvale...Why not write it down, to be sure."

Paul tapped his head. "Indelible."

"Eight o'clock, okay? I have to baby-sit my little brother that night, so it will be just perfect."

"Ah, baby-sitting, huh? So . . . does this little brother bite?"

"No, me." She started the car. "I'm the one who bites." She pulled out of the parking space and drove off.

Paul found his heart was pounding as he watched her drive off.

"Hey, guy, ya wanna heave that thing back?" one of the guys called, meaning the Frisbee.

"Yeah!" said Paul, feeling like a Greek god himself as he sailed it easily over their heads.

Chapter Seven

God, she was attractive!

Dr. John Mathewson sat in the Century 21 office, trying not to stare at this most curious specimen of female who was helping him in his quest for suitable quarters. Damn it! Why hadn't he worn some cologne? Had he even thought to comb his hair?

And shit, maybe his underarm deodorant was wearing off.

Thank God he'd taken a shower that morning!

"Could you spell that for me, Doctor?" the woman asked politely, wearing a most professional smile in her pretty, only slightly worn features.

L-u-s-t, thought Mathewson perversely.

"Right." He cleared his throat. "M-a-t-h-e-w-s-o-n. John Mathewson."

The woman looked at him with an unreadable expression. "And you're interested in a one-bedroom sublet, furnished—"

"Yes, that's correct," he said, gazing absently around the tastefully if modestly furnished office, complete with walls full of maps and certificates.

What was going on in her mind? Did she like him at all? Or did she just see a close-to-middle-age jerk wanting a hovel to squat in, while she dreamed of some muscle-bound hunk at home, primed for raw sex?

"Any special requirements?"

John nodded, able to concentrate on this bit. "It should be quiet..." He smiled. "And in an English-speaking country."

That earned a smile... alas, just a small smile.

"I think we can handle that." She glanced down at her form. "Children?"

"Not to my knowledge!" said John, with a canny laugh.

"Excuse me?" she said, a faint tone of annoyance in her voice.

"No. No children."

"Pets?"

"No pet, no children, no flamenco dancing..."

She raised her delicate eyebrows. "So it's just you and... er..."

"Just me and my books. And my memories, of course...."

She smiled.

No good. He had to admit it. He was smitten. Oh, how the mighty fall! A genius, a great man of science, felled by the wink of some tart!

She looked at him strangely, as though just seeing him for the first time, and suddenly it was as though they were two bulbs on a Van de Graaff generator, and a stream of electricity snapped across the gap....

Cripes!

She got up, and her hips moved provocatively beneath her skirt as she went to the file cabinet, pulled it open, and selected something from a folder.

"Well, let's see. It happens we have a very nice garden condominium that's on a sublet. New building, good neighborhood, near the university, five hundred a month including utilities..."

She moved back and handed him a brochure. John barely noticed the pictures and specifications printed on the thing... he was too wrapped up in observing the results of hormones spurting into his bloodstream.

Amazing!

"There's a list of particulars on the back—"

"No, that's okay." Rapid pulse. Increased perspiration. A sense of elation he hadn't felt for quite a time...

He handed the brochure back to her.

"You don't like it?"

"No! No, I love it. In fact, I'll take it!" he said, a note of glee in his voice.

"You'll take it?"

"Yes."

Her smile flip-flopped into an expression of amazement. "Just like that?"

"Uh-huh. I'm a very spurm...spur-of-the-moment kinda guy."

"Without even seeing it?"

"You said it was nice."

"Well...okay! Hey, that was easy."

"Oh," he said, "I'm very easy."

He leaned back in his seat, thinking, God, what am I saying? I don't even know if this woman is married or not. He didn't see a ring, but these days that didn't mean anything.

"Well, that should make completing these forms a really pleasant experience." She handed him the paper and a pen, and he set to work with a will.

He could feel her gaze upon him as he filled out the blanks. She shifted about uncomfortably, doing this and that while he made speedy work of the things.

"How curious," she said finally. "You don't have to consult anything for your numbers."

"Oh. Yes, that's right." He tapped his forehead. "I've got a gift for numbers, let's say. High retention." He jotted down his signature, then turned the papers back to her.

Peripherally, he heard the sound of a bike outside being chained to a post, then the pad of footsteps.

He turned, and saw a teenage boy enter...lanky, fair, in that formless teenage mold somewhere between boy and man, handsome with the surly glow of youth. Their gazes met, but Mathewson could read nothing in the expression. He shrugged, and turned to the much more interesting sight of the pretty real estate agent.

"I guess that does it, so..." She put her hand out. "Welcome to Ithaca, Dr. Mathewson."

He shook the hand, and it felt very nice indeed.

"If there's anything I can do..." she said.

John smiled with the same smile he had used on the government. "There is one thing."

"Yes?"

"This is going to sound terribly abrupt, but the thing is...I've been here for six weeks, down at the Carriage House Motel, and I don't know a soul in town, and you've been so nice...I thought perhaps some night you'd let me take you to dinner."

The teenager, meantime, had settled at a nearby computer terminal and was clicking away idly. But he paused a moment and eyed the couple curiously.

The woman's eyes opened wider. "It's...I can't, no—"

John smiled at lower wattage. "Really?"

"It's sweet of you, but—it's quite impossible."

"No, I understand. You've got something...well..." Small disappointed frown. Gets them every time... such a cute little-boy face he had! "If you'll excuse me, I'll go back to my room and see if they've rewrapped the soap...."

She smiled an oh-so-gentle smile. "It's not that bad, is it? Paul, come say hello." She beckoned. "This is my son Paul, Dr. Mathewson."

The teenager relinquished terminal duty, got up, and came over to his mother.

"Your— Oh! I didn't realize. I thought—this is terrible, I feel like a perfect ass—"

"Oh, nobody's *perfect,* Dr. Mathewson." She gave him a sly, cutting smile.

A wit! Touché! Damn, now he liked her twice as much! The lady had a head on her shoulders and a tongue in that head!

"I'm sorry." No, she wasn't, the smile said. "That wasn't called for. It's okay, really . . . my husband and I are divorced."

Mathewson felt a wave of relief sweep over him. "Oh! I mean . . ." He turned to Paul. "Hi, Paul. My name's John."

The woman was straightening his collar and was looking at him with great affection.

"Hello." And they shook hands.

They shook hands, and Paul's grip was precociously firm and assertive. As they greeted, Mathewson's eyes caught sight of Paul's notebook and schoolbooks stacked on top of a desk.

"Science buff?"

As Mathewson leaned over to check a book out, Paul shrugged noncommittally.

Mathewson flipped through the text, looking at some of the illustrations. Very familiar stuff, if quite primitive. "Lasers . . . fantastic things, lasers. Ever see one in the flesh?"

Paul blinked. "Not really."

"Well . . ." And a spectacular idea came to him, and he knew what Einstein must have felt like when the old MC got squared. "The funny coincidence is, I just happen to have access to one of the sexiest lasers in the entire free world, and if your mother says okay—" Boy, talk about brownie points! He picked out a small notebook from his breast pocket and wrote down a number—"you can come out to the lab and . . ."

See what's on the slab!

". . . and I'll give you the grand tour. Laser heaven." He raised an eyebrow worthy of Mr. Spock. "What do you say?"

He ripped out the loose-leaf paper and handed it to Paul. The guy was definitely intrigued, no question about that. Paul turned to his mother for a clue. Elizabeth seemed a little doubtful, but also seemed to enjoy this little ploy greatly.

"Well, I shouldn't like to stand in the way of Paul's education!" she said.

"A laser, huh? I made a laser once for a science project. Light amplification by stimulated emission of radiation."

"Ah yes, absolutely, Paul, but you haven't seen a real laser until you've laid your eyes on this baby!"

"Sure! When? I can't do it now, I have to go pick up some stuff."

His mother looked at him crossly. "You haven't gone to the Yateses' yet, Paul."

"I figured to give them a little more time."

"Then you'll be home late for dinner."

"Yeah."

There was a bit of solemn silence, and Mathewson wondered what the hell was going on.

"How about tomorrow afternoon about this time? Call during your lunch break to make sure, okay?"

"Yeah!" said Paul. "Yeah, why not!"

"Why not, indeed. Well, I hope to see you sometime again, Mrs. Stephens."

"I don't see how I'm going to be able to avoid it," she returned.

He did a double take at that one, but as he met her gaze he saw a lot more there than was immediately apparent in her voice.

With a smile, he bid farewell and went out to get himself a steak and ketchup dinner to celebrate.

Chapter Eight

It was a beautiful old house situated on the west side of College Town. At least a hundred years old, it stood amid poplars and oak like some regal statesman among his peers, the other beautiful houses that lined the thoroughfare.

Although it was late September, Indian summer was in full swing; the leaves were still green and the air was warm as Paul Stephens rode his bike up the new macadam driveway of the Yateses' house. The sun hung in the trees like some early Christmas bauble, and the evening was golden with it. Paul noted the immaculately manicured lawn and the neatly clipped hedges of this lovely estate as he parked his bike to one side of the garage and walked across the slate stones of the sidewalk. The odor of the new-cut lawn was in the air, along with the bright scent of the variety of flowers that grew in front of a huge picture window.

Ah yes, thought Paul, examining the neat placement of the azaleas and the morning glories. Yes, the American dream!

He rang the doorbell beside a perfect door, and it

chimed perfectly within the house, resonating deeply through the enormousness of it all.

The sound of steps, high heels most certainly, answered the call. The door opened. An attractively dressed woman with a string of pearls about a sleek neck looked out and smiled to see who was there.

"Paul!" she said. "I'm so glad you've come!"

"I'm sorry it's been a while," he said. "I figured I should wait a while." The familiar smell of well-scrubbed house, American style, wafted through. If cleanliness was next to godliness, then the Yates family was sitting right there at the Heavenly Gates!

"Yes... how thoughtful. But you could have come at any time, you know. Did you come with a car?"

"No. I put a basket on my bike."

"Paul... there's a lot of things!"

"Yes, but I'm only taking what... what I think that Richard would know I'd like to have."

She paused for a moment, and then nodded her graying head, perfectly styled.

"Very well. I... I know you know where the room is. I needn't show you. I don't like going there, as you can—" She got past the slight catch in her voice. "As you can imagine."

"No. You didn't much like going there when he was around either, though, did you?"

She shook her head sadly.

"All right. I won't be very long." He walked past her, down the corridor. In the study, through a partially opened door, he saw Dr. Yates sitting in his ancient armchair, reading the paper, perfectly poised, perfectly groomed, in perfect concentration. Yates was dean of the Science Division of Cornell at the age of fifty-five, a great accomplishment. He was a respected man of letters and of science, with credits the length of an arm for all manner of things, from army service to PTA service. Yes, a pillar of the community! A man of greatness! His first two sons were even now amazing their respective worlds of economics and medicine with their incredible acumen and money-gathering genius.

And the final son, of course, was six feet under, pumped up with formaldahyde.

Not bad, really. Statistically, in fact, it was very good, and Dr. Oliver Yates certainly appreciated statistics!

The old man sensed someone gazing at him and turned half-frames over to look at Paul, who gave him a silly grin and sped on his way.

And it was a familiar way indeed, since he and Richard Yates had been buddies since childhood. Down the Persian carpet! Up the stairs, sided and banistered with teak and walnut! Past scowling generations of Yates portraits, and a whole line of semipriceless works of art, down the hall, make a left, and through a door that had once held a Middle Earth poster, until the parental units had torn it down with much brouhaha.

Paul took a deep breath and opened the door.

They hadn't done anything to it yet, thank God. It still smelled of dirty socks and incense.

Paul walked in. It was a large room, natch, and it had years of teenage detritus arrayed in pure messy glory. The curtains were closed, and Paul went and opened them. The early-evening sunlight spilled through, illuminating the Richard Thompson poster first, above the headboard of Richard's bed.

Richard Thompson, most unlikely guitar hero there ever was.

He remembered the day at school when Richard had run excitedly up to him with a copy of the new *Rolling Stone*. "You won't believe it, Paul! *Rolling Stone* has an article about Richard Thompson. They call him the best rock guitarist in the world!"

"What happened to Eric Clapton and Eddie van Halen?"

Richard had made a face. "Pretty good article, too. Did you know that Linda Thompson once hit Richard over the head with a Coke bottle while they were in the midst of their divorce?"

"Hey, juicy stuff."

Richard shook his head. "Poor Richard."

"He should write an almanac."

Richard Thompson, of course, was the king of the Brit folk rockers. Back in the late sixties he and several other teenagers, long-haired hippies all, had started up a new kind of music: electrified folk. Well, it wasn't that new, really. The Byrds and Dylan had really started it, back in the U.S.A., with American folk music. The thing was that Brit folk, with its Celtic and European influences, was far, far weirder. Thompson along with some cronies, including Ashley Hutchings and Dave Swarbrick, had started the seminal folk-rock band, Fairport Convention. With the addition of the incredibly beautiful voice of Sandy Denny, they did some very nice music indeed, much of it traditional, some of it Thompson compositions. Thompson had gone on to do his own obscure solo albums, and more popular albums with wife Linda, but it was only in the eighties that the man's musical genius had gotten much attention from the mass media...mostly because of Thompson's own shyness of publicity, his lack of drive, and his infamous disdain for the fiscal spoils of musical fame.

Guitar hero...Richard Yates's hero, certainly.

Richard had both an acoustical and an electric guitar, both of which he practiced on constantly, usually playing folk-rock stuff. Paul would say to him, Why do Thompson when you can do Townsend or Clapton or Hendrix or stuff like that?

And Richard would just smile and say that it expressed what he felt much better....Oh, sure, he would slam out the occasional power chord to annoy his parents from time to time, but in the main he stuck to Brit stuff. He was even talking about taking up the fiddle so he could play jigs and reels, but he never did....Very hard, the fiddle.

Paul put his hands on his hips and looked around the room.

The predominant feature, of course, was the bookshelves and their bulging, sprawling, multitudinous books. All kinds of books. Richard had always been a voracious reader. A large portion, though, were science-fiction and fantasy books and digest-sized magazines. Lots of fantasy, detective novels, best-sellers (old Richard was a raving Stephen King fanatic; maybe he wouldn't have offed himself if he knew, as Paul had recently learned, that there were going to be four—count 'em, *four*—new King novels next year. Maybe he would have stuck around for those!), et cetera, et cetera.

Paul walked over to the shelves and looked at the middle one.

In the last year, Richard Yates had become somewhat of a collector of books—nonfiction and fiction—about nuclear war. Yep, and here they were, from *Warday* to *Truly Tasteless Jokes about Nuclear War*.

Paul took down the latter and thumbed through it.

There, at the end of all the sick and nasty jokes, was a quote from the *British Military Manual*, 1949: "The best defense against an atom bomb is not to be there when it goes off."

Paul laughed and put the book back.

Yeah, Richard Yates had this intense fascination with nuclear war.... He'd told Paul that it was only a matter of time before some Libyan or PLO terrorist figured out how to put one together....

And lately, he'd been going around with a haunted look, saying that it was only a matter of time before humanity blew itself off the face of the earth, and we'd better do it real quick, or we'll do a technologically superior job by the turn of the millennium, truly removing any shred of evidence that we'd troubled the universe with our evolving genes.

After Richard had stopped the progress of his own genes, Paul had gone to a shrink. First, to help himself with his own guilt. And also to try to understand.

The shrink was helpful with the first bit.

And he'd also made sense when he suggested that Richard's obsession with the oncoming holocaust was simply a projection of his own psychological distress, which had nothing to do with nuclear war.

But Paul wasn't so sure about that.

Thing was, you look at the facts—the facts that Richard presented to him, the facts that were available to everybody—and things looked pretty damned bad. Here were two stubborn superpowers with paranoid leaders just itching for some kind of fight. But the trouble was, each had in its hands weapons that would not only kill the enemy, but it as well. Still, the itch was there, and with the general brainpower of each about enough to run a fifteen-watt bulb, pure aggressive instincts seemed likely to overcome anything like reason and desire for the species to survive.

"Oh yes," Richard would say. "The species is going to be feces!"

Paul would argue with him, sometimes violently. He agreed with all the facts, sure. What Paul could not fathom was this idiotic pessimism rampant among youth.

"Oh yeah, sure, Mr. Sunshine!" Richard would say mordantly. "Just what can the youth of America do? I mean, I could give a shit about the threat of Communism in the world...and most of the products of our cultural system don't even know what Communism is....They just think they're the Nazi-sounding guys who tortured Sylvester Stallone in *Rambo*. I mean, it's even getting worse these days. Colleges seem to be regurgitating brainwashed puppies whose sense of history was entirely learned in their capitalist business classes! Nope, it's like the punks were saying in 1977. No future!"

"They were talking about pop culture, Richard. You know, Culture Club, Wham!, Duran Duran. No future there!"

Richard had just shaken his head. "You're just bringing me down more, man!" And he went to put on a Battlefield Band album.

"I guess...I guess most kids...hell, most people feel helpless. They think, what can you do, write to your congressman? Well, I say, sure! Every little bit helps!"

"Oh sure. A little bit of paper against a firestorm!"

"Well, damn it, I'll do something if I can!"

"What are you going to do? We're all going to get nuked, Paul! We're going to get nuked, and I'd do something too. . . ." He stared straight ahead of him as the plaint of tin whistles and flutes sweetened the dour air. "I'd do anything."

So, thought Paul, attention back to the present, back to this room chock-full of memories.

Do it, and get the hell out of here!

He found a cardboard box in the closet, and he selected some albums from the huge stack (Richard, for all of his eschewing of capitalism, certainly enjoyed using his capitalist father's money!). He took the ones especially valuable, the first pressings of the Steeleye Span albums and the Fairports, some Martin Carthy, some Pentangle. He had lots of the others already, but Richard would definitely have wanted him to have these.

From the bookshelf he selected a few of Richard's favorites, including a Stephen King first edition of *Carrie* he'd managed to get signed. The sucker was worth a thousand bucks now, easy, but Paul sure as hell wasn't going to sell it.

He lingered just a moment over the nuclear section. There it was! The *Plutonium Handbook*. A rare little number indeed, and wouldn't Wilke be surprised with some of the stuff old underachiever Stephens was going to come up with soon in class!

Anarchists, unite!

Smiling to himself, Paul checked out Richard's comic collection, got a stack of the really good stuff the guy had collected (thirty comics, worth about twenty thou . . . old man Yates had never fathomed this at all, and he and Richard used to laugh when they would show him a copy of *Spiderman No. 1* and announce it was worth at least fifteen hundred bucks).

The box was getting full. Room for not much more.

He went to the closet, got out Richard's acoustic guitar. He could strap that around his back, no problem.

What else?

Paul went to Richard's desk, and he knew what else, immediately.

He looked at the thing, and he sat down in the chair, and looked at it some more.

About five years ago, an itinerant carnival had come to town, complete with rinky-dink roller coaster. They'd gone, of course, Richard and he had, daredevil eleven years old they, and they'd ridden that roller coaster lots. At the highest peak, on a post, had been a sign reading DON'T STAND UP.

A pretty bright idea, that. Richard had been fascinated with that sign, and he had noted that the roller coaster was constructed like a Tinkertoy, easily climbable. After closing, one night, by moonlight, they had climbed up and, with the help of Paul's mechanical expertise, they had gotten Richard's sign for him.

Richard, sitting on that roller coaster track, had looked up at the sky, had said, "The stars, Paul! Look at 'em all. We're going to get there someday, mankind. I really believe that!"

Paul had just wanted to get down, before they got caught.

So he took the sign off the wall in front of the desk, the one that said DON'T STAND UP in bright red letters, and he held it in his lap, and he couldn't stop the tears anymore.

"Oh, Richard," he sighed. "You asshole."

Chapter Nine

Paul Stephens pedaled along the country road atop his blue bike, upon which he'd painted a red speed-stripe. Not that the thing went all that fast. Paul just thought the addition looked rather snazzy and suited his personality. He could do all kinds of weird stunts on this bike; he'd used his mechanical abilities to take it apart and put it back together to precisely suit his sense of balance.

He'd always had the mechanical gift; the chemical genius had arrived later, or at least been exposed later, when, at age eleven, the departed elder Mr. Stephens, he of the wandering gonads and the handsome dash, had given him a very large, very expensive chemistry set for his birthday. That whole summer had been full of strange odors rising up from the cellar, to say nothing of the frequent explosions and strange tinge to Paul's skin. But after all was said, done, and blown up, Paul Stephens emerged from that summer basement with an odd command of things chemical to add to his knack with things physical.

And dear Dad, astonished at the range of his abilities, had just shaken that *GQ* head, taken the cigar from between his lips, and asked, "How do you do it, Paul?"

And Paul had answered, "Elementally, my dear chap!"

Yeah, thought Paul, tooling along on the macadam road. Dad was really okay, even though he hated his guts on principle. In fact, Paul had been thinking lately about calling the guy up. Father–son crap. Try and talk about Richard.

Maybe.

But for now, he was going to get a look at this place Dr. Mathewson worked at. Lasers were most interesting things, and Paul had always had a fascination with them. The chance of looking at a really serious one was too good an opportunity to pass up.

There was a signpost up ahead, which read MED-ATOMICS, and a little way down the road was a security station by the appropriate gate. As Paul pulled up to it he noticed that a surveillance camera was focused on his every move.

Figures moved behind glass.

"Please state your name and business," declared a small speaker horn, sounding almost human.

"Uh, yeah. Paul Stephens. Dr. Mathewson is expecting me."

A moment for a check. Meantime, Paul did a quick scan of the security setup. Yeah. Real sophisticated. Doubtless, somewhere deep in the guts of this place a computer sat like a spider at the middle of its web, watching, watching. And now this security/receptionist was picking up a phone to check to see if this here teenager was speaking the truth.

"Thank you," said the speaker horn.

And the gates opened. Paul rode through to the main entrance.

A streak of white.

Was was that?

A rabbit dashed through the open gate, out into freedom. An escaped lab animal? Paul laughed and wished it well.

Riding up to the building, he noticed the doc's

snazzy Mercedes parked in front of the low-slung main building. How did a scientist make enough money to afford something like that car, unless he was Carl Sagan? Curious, that.

Paul skipped up some steps, entered the lobby, where an attractive woman asked him to sign in and handed him a film badge and a bright red visitor's badge.

"Radioactive?" Paul asked.

The receptionist smiled. "You'd better hope not! 'Course, if it were, I sure wouldn't be here!"

"No Karen Silkwood, huh?"

"No way, José." She indicated a door. "That's the way you go, my friend. Have a good time with Dr. Mathewson. He's a real character."

"I think he wants to get into my mom's..." Paul smiled. "Affections!"

"Ah. Well, it's nice to know the man has normal drives. Lately, he's been putting a lot of time in here. But you'll get along. He really is a nice guy."

"Thanks."

By the door stood a lab attendant, a sandy-haired fellow.

"Hi. I'm George Samuels. Dr. Mathewson asked me to collect you."

"I'm all signed in. Let's go."

They went down a hallway. Further down, two corridors formed a T.

Paul looked up at the ceiling at some devices hanging down.

"What are those?" he asked.

"Motion detectors," answered the lab attendant.

Paul nodded and stared at them a moment. "Damned sophisticated."

"Oh yes," said the attendant glibly. "We're very proud of our motion detectors."

They were in a radiation detection room now, Paul realized. They proceeded through a radiation detector built into the door that led to another lab corridor. Paul noticed the radiation device, and looked up at the bright red sign above it.

WARNING, it read. DANGER. RADIATION.

Sure. Real safe here.

What the hell are they *really* doing? a little nagging voice said in the back of his mind.

And down the corridor some more, to windows showing the main lab area.

What an amazing collection of machines! Totally *amazing!* Dials and knobs and computer screens! Oh boy, oh boy, thought Paul, his mechanical sense of wonder kicking in like clockwork.

Samuels opened the door with a key-card. Paul noted that although you needed one of these things to get in, it was the kind of lock where you could get out without one. Curious.

Paul went through, and the full impact hit him, and he could not hide his awe.

The very air seemed charged with an electrical excitement of highly evolved computers and equipment meshed into a helter-skelter of scientific investigation. Imagination and knowledge made steel and glass and power! Even the air smelled faintly of the electricity that throbbed through these wonderful toys of the mind like testosterone through a nineteen-year-old's brain.

And there he stood, Master of Mystery. Doc Mathewson, his baby face intent, his eyes a touch wild, his hair unkempt. What an interesting man!

As though sensing that someone was staring at him, he looked around and he saw Paul.

A broad smile split his features. He hurried over and shook hands and said, "So glad you could make it, Paul. Thanks, Samuels, I think I can take over now."

Samuels nodded and took off.

"Yes. I do believe I promised to show you some lasers, correct?"

Paul nodded.

John did just that. A few casual explanations and steps later, they were standing by a small laser setup consisting of a tube about two feet long and some auxiliary equipment. John switched the thing on, and Paul glanced over to where technicians were working on a humongous version of this model of a laser-isotope setup.

Boy, talk about microcosm-macrocosm!

He sure wished he could play with that one up there, and he said as much to Dr. Mathewson.

"Little leagues first, I'm afraid, Paul. But I don't think you'll be disappointed with this demonstration. Now watch."

Mathewson flicked a switch. A pencil beam of blue-green suddenly existed where there had been only air before.

"And—" continued John.

The scientist placed his hand in front of the beam, then took it away.

"Amplified light, Paul, as you know. . . . Go ahead, you give it a try. It's perfectly safe now."

Paul put his hand in front of the beam, feeling nothing but a tingle of excitement. He took the hand away, and checked it to make sure there wasn't a hole burned into it.

"Right. But now let's heat things up a bit. Would you put these on? We're going to go a bit further than rock-video power."

He handed Paul a pair of goggles and slipped a set on himself. Then he turned a dial.

Goggles on, Paul turned back and saw that the light was indeed much brighter.

"Feel like a smoke?" asked Dr. Mathewson. He took a cigar from his pocket and placed it in the beam. The end began smoldering; lit brightly. Paul's nostrils cringed with the smell. He hated cigars. His dad used to smoke them.

Then Mathewson took a special mirror from a set of several, then clamped a half-inch steel plate into a vise and adjusted the mirror so it reflected the laser onto the steel.

"Now, this is the kind of thing I think you really came to see, Paul." Mathewson's eyes gleamed strangely in the light from the laser beam as he set

the laser to PULSE mode. With a droning kind of
whine, the machine built up power and—

Bam!

Sparks flew about, and smoke drifted up.

Unable to help himself, Paul flinched back.

"What do you think?" Mathewson said proudly.
God, the guy looked like a kid with a favorite toy.

Something was dancing on Paul's spine. This was
damned impressive! Imagine what that big mother
up there could do!

"Not bad," he said.

"Not bad?" Mathewson said. "Not bad! I've just
cut through a steel plate with a beam of light, and
he says, not bad."

Sarcastically.

Damn. I like this guy, but I sure don't *want* to!

"C'mon, then," said Mathewson. "Maybe I can show
you some other stuff that you might approve of."

Paul found himself being ushered down the main
corridor.

Dr. Mathewson's finger was doing a great deal of
pointing.

"Main reaction chamber here," he said, pointing
to a huge machine. "Vaccum assembly . . . assay area
over there . . . robot runs the whole thing. . . . So . . . tell
me." He turned to look at him seriously. "What does
he do for a living? Your old man."

"Hmm? Oh yeah. He taught architecture at Cornell." His eyes had been attracted by something.
"What's that?"

Very curious indeed! Here was an area where
stacked together were many bottles of green gel, with
sparkles in them, like exotic hairstyling gunk.

"Uhmm . . . where?" asked Mathewson, playing coy.

"Back there."

"Oh yes, there. Why, that's . . . ah . . . lubricating oil,
I guess. For the robot. Oh my . . . look at the time.
Come on, I'll walk you out."

"Sure. Thanks."

Outside, divested of his visitor's and film badges,
Paul walked for his bike, Mathewson at his side.

They passed a sign reading CAUTION—HIGH VOLT-
AGE—UNDERGROUND CABLE.

Mathewson broke the silence. "So where is he now?
Your father, I mean."

"Oh. He's in Saudi Arabia. Hotshot job."

"Really? What happened?"

Nosy guy!

Paul looked at him and spoke in a terse voice. "I
guess you could say he didn't like being married."

Mathewson's eyes looked up to the sky, as though
searching for God in heaven. "Some people don't know
when they're well off."

"Actually, he's a brilliant architect. Just kind of
a shit in his personal life." He gave Mathewson a
cagey look. "You gonna go out with Elizabeth?"

"Elizabeth?"

"My mother."

Paul knelt down and tied his sneaker. As he worked
on the laces, he saw something in the grass.

Huh?

He looked closer as Mathewson moved on a few
steps, looking out over a lake, sucking in some fresh
air.

"Oh, right...Elizabeth. I guess that's up to her.
She's certainly an unusual woman, don't you think?"

Good grief! How could this be?

"Paul?"

Paul picked something out of the grass and looked
back at the research facility.

What kind of place is this, for God's sake?

"Excuse me?"

"Your mother."

"Oh, right. Yeah," said Paul Stephens. "Very unusual."

Jesus, he thought, looking down at the five-leaf
clover.

And it wasn't a curse. It was a prayer.

Chapter Ten

Dr. John Mathewson was telling a joke.

"What's the hot new venereal disease amongst Jewish American princesses?" he asked Paul and Elizabeth.

Elizabeth was still laughing at the last one. "I haven't the faintest," she said, hanging on to her large goblet of wine as though she were afraid it might disappear.

"MAIDS," said Mathewson. "They just *die* if they don't have one!"

Elizabeth laughed harder, her cheeks getting red.

Dumb, thought Paul. Really *dumb!*

They sat in a cozy booth at the best restaurant in town, Gustav's. Candlelight, music, wine ... delectable food. The works! This guy, thought Paul, this mad scientist, is certainly not stinting on his efforts to seduce my mother.

And I've got to watch!

Couldn't really blame him, though. Mom sure did look lovely today. Alive. Really enjoying herself, in her nice dress and her new hairstyle. And now she seemed to really glow with the wine and the warm lighting, and with this attention from a guy she clearly liked.

God, it was tough being a son of an attractive unattached mother!

John Mathewson hailed a waiter and tapped the empty bottle of Bordeaux sitting among the remnants of an outrageous dinner.

"Oh, John. No more for me. My head is spinning."

"Good for the head to spin, keeps it stable.... Come on, Paul. You haven't touched yours."

Paul glared at his wine. "No, thank you, I don't drink wine."

"Paul! Why? You like your British beer!" said Elizabeth, clearly pleasantly high.

"Wine impairs my judgment," Paul said.

"Really," said his mother lightly.

"Would you two excuse me a moment?" said Mathewson. "Nature calls..."

"Certainly," said Elizabeth brightly.

As soon as Mathewson left, Paul turned to his mother.

"You don't really like this creep, do you?"

"Creep! Paul, he's very nice! I haven't had such a nice date for a long time...and you know it." She patted his hand lightly. "Just you worry about your own love life, and leave mine alone, okay? What, are you nervous about Jenny tonight?"

"Tonight? Oh...yeah. No. I guess I'm not nervous."

"The cutest girl in your chem lab, and you're not nervous? What's wrong with you, Paul?"

"I don't know," said Paul morosely. But he did know.

She sipped at her wine. "Paul. Are you jealous?"

"Oh yeah. I wanna kill Dad and marry you and have kids and then punch my eyes out!"

"I'm really flattered, but maybe we should talk."

Paul sighed. "Look. I'm just sick of a lot of things, Mom. Maybe I'm just going through a phase. I'm just really...angry!"

"Mmm. And so I see! And you're so cute when

you're angry. I think you should stay that way. Jenny sounds like a girl who might like that!"

"What are you talking about?"

Elizabeth, it seemed, had had even more wine than he realized. "How about a little bit of mother–son talk? Your dad's not around, so maybe I should clue you in on something."

"Clue. Huh?"

"A little-girlie secret, Paul. If you and Jenny should get in a clinch...I mean, you know, make out..." Her eyes widened a bit, glistening. "Be firm!"

"What?"

"Be manly! You've got to be more manly to turn girls on. You know, dominant. I think sometimes fey little Richard was a bad influence on you."

"Domination!" said Paul angrily. "I'd like to kill the ape that invented male domination!"

"That's right, dear. You've got the spirit."

Paul opened his mouth to say something more, but decided against it. He was so deeply angry he almost shoved the clovers in her stupid face.

But he restrained himself, and almost instantly John Mathewson was back.

Elizabeth smiled up at him, and Paul could read submission all over her face, and he wanted to take a steak knife and ram it through this smiling mad-man's heart.

"Hmmm!" Elizabeth said, shivering. "Seems to have gone cold in here!"

"Here," said Mathewson obligingly. "Take my jacket!"

"No. You'll be cold then too. Paul, I left my sweater in Dr. Mathewson's car. Would you be a sweetheart and go out and get it?"

"Sure," said Paul, and he knew she was getting rid of him, and it was fine by him because he was about ready to barf if he stayed here any longer.

He went outside, into the growing dusk, to Dr. Mathewson's Mercedes. He opened the door and got his mother's sweater, which was lying on the front seat.

He noticed the car's glove compartment.

Hmm.

Maybe it was time for the old lock-pick trick. Yes, definitely. Trouble was, he didn't have anything to pick it with.

He checked inside his mother's purse. Here we go. He pulled out a barrette with a metal clip. Good enough.

It was but the work of a short moment to get the thing open. Inside the glove compartment was a leather thing. A billfold kind of affair, real fancy. Paul picked it out, had a look.

Inside were a cluster of ID cards and similar stuff. Paul leafed through them.

DEPARTMENT OF ENERGY, said one.

PAN TEX, said another.

And more. OAK RIDGE NATIONAL LABORATORIES. LOS ALAMOS LABORATORIES. LIVERMORE NATIONAL LABORATORIES. Y-12/UNION CARBIDE.

More identification, security badges...

And that key-card.

On the key-card was a picture of Dr. John Mathewson below a MedAtomics logo.

Wow, and double wow, thought Paul, staring at this.

He didn't do it very long, though. He wiped off his fingerprints, using his Mom's sweater, and replaced everything just as he had found it.

He gazed around, making sure no spook or government flunky was watching him.

Whew.

He slammed the glove compartment, got out of the Mercedes, and went back into Gustav's, a thoughtful expression on his face.

There was a bit of hallway beside the booth where his mother and Dr. Mathewson were sitting, and he paused for a moment where they couldn't see him. He listened to what they were saying.

"I'm drunk," said Elizabeth.

"Just a little. Do you remember putting the salad bowl on your head?"

Paul heard his mother giggle, and his heart sank.

"So what kind of doctor are you anyway, Doctor?" she asked.

Doctor bloody Frankenstein, fumed Paul.

"Not the kind that makes house calls."

"A dermatologist?"

"No, no...research. Um...medical research."

"How noble. Have you discovered the cure for anything?"

"Not yet."

Paul turned the corner, handed his mother the sweater. She draped it over her shoulders.

"Better?" asked John.

"Mmm. Thank you, sweetheart."

Paul looked down uneasily at John Mathewson. "Thank you very much for dinner. It was very stimulating."

"You leaving already? What about dessert?"

"Sorry, I have a date."

"Yes. A very cute girl, John." She patted his arm lovingly. "You two have a good time."

"Yeah," said Paul, and he left, his mind spinning like some crazy top.

Chapter Eleven

Paul Stephens, when he walked up the steps to the rambler house Jenny Anderman lived in, was in a haze of preoccupation, precariously balanced between anger and despair.

He pounded on the front door.

She opened it. "Hi, Paul!" And she looked absolutely ravishing in a soft blue ruffled blouse, tight Calvin Klein jeans, and hair waved with just the right touch of sass.

"Hi," Paul muttered, and he walked into the house as though it were a funeral parlor.

"Just on time," said Jenny brightly. God, she thought. He doesn't seem to notice the bottle of Opium I drenched myself with! "Um...have a seat in the family room. Want a Coke or something?"

"Yeah." He went and sat down in the adjacent room. It was scattered with toys of amazing variety, and occupied also by a little boy with the devil in his eyes, wearing a Cornell Law School sweatshirt.

"Paul, this is Barnaby, my brother."

"Hi, Barnaby."

"Shit!" said Barnaby, grabbing a nearby He-Man

doll and throwing it violently against the fireplace grate. "Shit! Shit!"

"Kid trying to tell us something?" Paul murmured.

"No. Daddy just watched a PG-13 movie today, and Barnaby learned some new words."

"Great."

Barnaby proceeded to gnaw on the head of Rainbow Brite.

"You've got to watch Barnaby, though. We had beans for dinner, and that always makes him hyper."

Paul grunted, wondering what kinds of beans, and about their particular explosive qualities when combined with the chemicals of a male youngster's digestive tract.

"Well, I see you brought your books. I've got mine right here." She tapped the chem books on the coffee table, right by the prerequisite Cornell supply of the season's coffee-table books. "I've got the new Rick Springfield album. Want me to put it on the stereo?"

Paul made a sour face.

"Shit!" cried Barnaby. "Shit!"

"You said it, kid," said Paul.

"Um ... maybe I should put on MTV instead. That would amuse Barnaby, and we could keep it low, so we can study."

"Fine," said Paul, leaning back morosely against the plush cushions. He was staring down at Barnaby, who was busy transforming a transformer into bits and pieces, hardly paying any attention to her at all.

He sure looked cute, though, when he frowned. Like, real grown-up and everything!

"Right. I'll go and get your Coke."

Troubled, Jenny went into the kitchen. She stared into a mirror by the fridge. Nope. No new zits. Was there stuff coming out of her nose or hanging from her teeth?

Nope.

She lifted her arm and sniffed. Deodorant was still working fine.

She looked at herself in the mirror, and suddenly

she wasn't the cute and strikingly made-up vixen that had been in the bathroom mirror before Paul had come over.

What was wrong?

Guys who came over for "studying"—any guy who got within striking distance of her missiles of scent and allure—usually started either to drool or to stutter. That was cool. She could handle that. She was in control then. Maybe she'd let them touch her a bit, kiss her a bit, but that was it. She was a good girl, after all, and she liked guys pawing her fine, but she knew where to draw the line. The big thrill was the control she had over the situation, watching the oafs get red-faced and humiliated. She got a sense of power. But this guy ... She liked this guy, and her usual ploys weren't ...

God, she hated the way she looked anyway!

She turned away from the mirror and went to get the drinks, getting Cokes, one for herself too, to hell with her complexion, she needed it.

When she got back, Paul was in the exact same position, only Barnaby was crawling on him.

"I think Barnaby thinks I'm his new toy," Paul said.

You were *supposed* to be mine, thought Jenny, putting the drinks down and grabbing her little brother. "You little menace, Paul's our guest!"

"I like him!" said Barnaby.

"Well, yeah, he's a nice guy. I guess."

"That's okay. I like kids. I'm sorry if I'm a touch on the grumpy side tonight, Jenny. There's just a lot going on inside my head, I guess."

That's not where it's supposed to be going on when you're around me, thought Jenny, but she found herself smiling understandingly, just like her mom did after Dad's "bad day" at work. "That's okay."

"Thanks for inviting me here. It's helping already."

Yeah, sure, Jenny thought. He's looking at me like I'm a dead fish or something. Maybe if I accidentally stuck my breast in his face or something...

"So...chemistry..."

Absolutely *none* so far, thought Jenny ruefully.

"Look," she said, with a soulful gaze. Mom again. "I don't think you're going to be able to study until you get this off your chest!" she said. "I'm a good listener, Paul, and God knows I get in a snit sometimes."

Paul was quiet for a moment, intensely thoughtful, and suddenly Jenny was ashamed of herself. Something more was going on inside this guy's head besides faulty football scores or a flat tire on his bike.

This guy had something real...deep...going on. This guy was...what was the term Daddy used? Yeah. Dimensional!

"I dunno if I should...."

"Paul! You've got to tell somebody!"

"No. No, I can't...it's too...too much." The pain was clear on his face.

"Okay. Whatever. Let's talk about something else, then."

She got out one of her mom's old Beatle records and played it, and they talked, and the talk went well. He still didn't seem to give a heck that she was female, but they honestly seemed to have the ability to relate to one another, which was rather astonishing. They talked about school and about Mr. Wilke and about Paul's taste in music (weird, but interesting), and Paul answered her questions about him, and she answered his about her...

And time slipped by, without much study.

"You want another drink?" she asked.

"How about something healthy? Got some orange juice?"

"Sure."

"Look, I'm enjoying talking to you. You're...you're real smart, Jenny. Fun."

"Thanks!"

"Yeah. I think I...trust you. Instinct, I suppose."

"Thank you. I feel flattered."

"I do have to talk, Jenny. I'm very upset."

"I won't tell a soul."

They went to get the orange juice while Barnaby played with a remote-control truck, slamming it joyfully through a bunch of dolls Paul had set up for him.

Paul told his story.

Jenny listened.

It sure was quite a story, all right!

Still...

"So what?" she said. "Plutonium. It's, like, just an element on the chart, isn't it?"

Paul had gotten a great deal more animated in his speech, and now he was gesturing with his hands as she was getting the orange-juice concentrate out of the refrigerator.

"Look! There are only two uses in the world for plutonium. In reactors and in weapons, right? Okay. So. If they're making reactors, why do they say it's medical? And if it's medical, why are they fooling around with plutonium? It just doesn't make any sense!"

She was opening the can of concentrate. She had the top off the can, but the goddamn stuff wouldn't come out. She shook it. Nothing. She stuck a knife in. Flakes.

"Here."

Paul took the can, found a church key, and opened a hole in the bottom. The slab of concentrate slid easily into the blender.

"Thanks. Just a moment, though, Paul. How do you know it's plutonium? Maybe it's something else—"

"It's not. It's little flakes of plutonium in this green gel. That's called a scintillant. I read about it in this book I got from this friend of mine."

Jenny shook her head. "But why would he just invite you inside? It's crazy!"

"So he's crazy. Look what he does for a living.... He's hot for my mother, I'm a dumb kid— Okay, Barnaby...give the bear a break," Paul called through the door.

Barnaby was whacking the stuffing out of a teddy bear with a Godzilla doll.

"Would you go out and stop him, Paul?" asked Jenny.

"Sure."

Inside the family room, the TV was blaring with a Muppets show, which Barnaby was ignoring. The sound of the blender added its whine to the ruckus.

Paul talked above the noise.

"Plus which, he's got all these IDs, security clearances, I don't know what they are. Los Alamos, Livermore labs, Oak Ridge. You know what they make at Oak Ridge?"

Jenny entered with juice for them all, Barnaby's in a spigot bottle.

"What?"

"Nuclear warheads."

"So what are you saying?"

"I'm saying he lied, okay? At the very least. He invites me out there and then he lies, like I'm some kind of *wimp*..."

"Are you sure you're not overreacting?"

"To what?"

"I dunno. Maybe it's... what did my psych teacher call it? Oedipal jealousy."

His eyes flared and Jenny caught her breath at the fury in him.

"Yeah, great... oedipal jealousy.... Look at this."

He dragged something out of his pocket.

"What is it?"

"What does it look like?"

She took it and examined it in better light. "Hey. It's a five-leaf clover. Where'd you find this?"

"Growing outside that lab. You know the odds on that kind of mutation happening naturally? Without chemicals or radiation or something?"

"What?"

"There are none. I looked it up. It's like a billion to one. It never happens."

"Maybe you're just very lucky!"

Paul dipped into his pocket again, opened his hand.

In it were dozens of five-leaf clovers.

Jenny stared at them a moment.

The reality began to sink in.

"Oh, my God," she said, shaken. "We should tell somebody."

"Who?"

"I dunno. A newspaper. Somebody. My father. I mean, you can't just waltz into a town and set up a ...a bomb factory next to people's houses!"

"It's not a factory. It's a laboratory."

"What's the difference? It's nuclear. You have to have hearings, you have to let the community know about it. There are laws!"

Suddenly she'd forgotten all about this stupid teenage sex business. Now she was in much older territory. From the time she could first remember, she recalled her father ranting about people standing up for their rights. Daddy was a lawyer at Cornell, and he had always been proud that his little girl's first complete sentence had been "Impeach Nixon!" after a rally he had taken her to. And Mom ...Mom had joined about every liberal cause there was from Amnesty International to the Live AID concert. Her study was still practically papered with posters from the sixties and early seventies.

"One thing, though, Jenny," he said, looking at her intently, as though seeing her for the first time.

She shivered slightly at this new attention.

"Oh?"

"It's a government lab. They're not gonna let anybody in there to look around."

"They let you in."

"Fluke. The guy was horny, he took a chance."

But Jenny was off, and her mother's blood inside her was aflame. "So we do nothing, is that it?"

"What do you want to do, march on Washington?"

"My parents happen to have met at a march on Washington."

"Really. How very sixties. Were you born at a Stones concert?"

Jenny was incensed.

"It's not funny. You know what this is like? It's like when you read about, I don't know, Anne Frank or something. And you say, Jesus, why didn't they *do* something? The whole world was collapsing and they just sat around, life as usual, thinking maybe it would go away. But it never goes away, it only gets worse, and nobody thinks about the future—"

"I know somebody who did."

"Who?"

"My best friend. Richard Yates. The guy with the plutonium book and a lot of other stuff on nuclear war."

"So what did *he* do about it?"

"Oh. He killed himself."

"You mean...oh yeah...I heard about that guy. ...Didn't go over the gorge...shot himself."

"Yeah."

"I'm so sorry."

"Yeah."

"Son of the dean of the Science Division, the paper said. At Cornell. Had lots of stuff...um...are you saying that he was freaked about nuclear war so he just..."

"Oh, that was a part of it, I guess. But there's more...more than any of us will ever know. That's the thing with the people that off themselves...you'll never know completely why."

"And I guess you feel guilty?"

"You bet."

"So why do you think, Paul?" she said softly.

"Like, you know, Cornell students dive off the bridge into the gorge every year. Only much more complex, and much worse."

"I guess having a father like that...a lot of pressure."

"A complete bastard, Jenny. Mr. American Achievement. And you know, the crazy thing was... I think...well, it's just a theory."

"So go ahead, Paul."

"Well, Dr. Yates had two other sons who have gone on to amazing success. And the thing is, that Richard

... Richard was smarter than all of them. I mean, IQ tests right off the map, and he had the most incredible imagination.... Sheesh, the guy clued me into so much... so much. But his grades... terrible! He was just always so bored at school. Own little world."

"Ah. And his father wasn't pleased."

"I think you can use your imagination on that.... But then make it even worse. Yates just rode Richard ... all the time. He used to taunt the poor guy.... I mean, once I heard him suggest that maybe the milkman had knocked up Mrs. Yates, because Richard sure wasn't *his* son!"

"God! Sounds like Richard should have shot his father, not himself!"

"Yeah. But you didn't know Richard. He loved his father very deeply, and admired him... and, gosh, I guess he wanted... he wanted the bastard to care for him too. He couldn't do something like rebel... not actively anyway. I mean, everybody else adores Dr. Yates. Humanitarian extremus, blah blah blah."

"So he thought we were going to get blown up, huh?"

"Sure did. Obsessed with it. And you know, his dad... his dad has worked with the CIA. The fucking spooks! Jesus!"

He sat down in a chair.

"Dad has a liquor cabinet. You want a drink?"

"No."

"Look, are you okay? I hate this government too, if that helps any."

"Yeah, I can tell." Lightning flashed outside the window, and Paul watched it, fascinated. "You know, just this year, start of summer, Richard and I were out in this field... and it was getting to be dusk... and all that stuff was going on in the Middle East ... hairy stuff. Anyway, toward the east, there were these flashes... heat lightning.

"So Richard... Richard just freezes, and he looks like he's seen a ghost. And he grabs my arm and says, 'You know, Paul,' he says, 'you're my best friend and I love you like my brother.' The guy thought the old warheads were going off."

"Woooo."

"And you know what I did? Maybe I'm as much of a bastard as his father, because I made fun of him."

Paul stared at the darkness with a haunted look. "I never told him that he was like a brother to me, too. That..."

He let the sentence drift.

"You're not a bastard, Paul. Not at all," she said quietly.

Lightning flashed again. Thunder roared.

Paul suddenly smiled. He got up and went to the window.

"The storm!" he said. "There's a storm coming!"

"So?"

And he felt like the idea was sticking the hammer of Thor in his hands.

"The lab! They got a security system there. TV cameras, motion detectors. All kinds of stuff. But it's all electric!"

"So?"

"Lightning!" Paul said, overjoyed. "Don't you see, Jenny? *Lightning!* Don't you get what I'm saying?"

"God's going to destroy the bad guys?"

"No," he said, chuckling. "We can get in there!" His eyes were wild with a kind of thrill that thrilled Jenny too, deeper than she had ever been thrilled before. "I mean, if you want to! I'd need your help."

What a crazy guy, thought Jenny Anderman. What a crazy wonderful guy this Paul Stephens is.

And she smiled at him, and her eyes got wild too.

Chapter Twelve

The radiation from the TV flickered upon the Anderman coffee table, recently denuded of fashionable coffee-table books.

In place of fancy books, these items now stretched out across the sheened walnut surface:

— Barnaby's remote control truck, complete with remote control devices;
— two Frisbees, top sides taped with discs of aluminum foil;
— a pair of dishwashing gloves;
— some plastic food-storage bags, about fifteen inches on a side;
— a small flashlight.

Also upon this impromptu lab area glinted scissors, Scotch tape, a bottle of the type of glitter used in kiddie craft projects.

Incredible what you can come up with from household knickknacks if you're a genius like me! thought Paul Stephens, engaged in shaking a quart bottle of liquid green detergent, into which he had just poured some of Barnaby's glitter.

He held it up to the light.

How scintillating!

"Here we go. My camera. Thirty-five millimeter," Jenny said, coming downstairs. "I knew I'd find it if I looked hard enough!"

She put the camera down and lit up a Merit 100 cigarette.

"That's very bad for you," Paul said.

"Yeah. So's breaking into secret government headquarters. Lots of stuff is bad for you. I hear that a bout of hetereosexuality recently almost did poor Boy George in!"

Paul went to her. "Gee. Poor guy."

"New York spree. Booze and women. Had to go through London Heathrow customs with a bag over his head, he looked so bad."

He took the cigarette from her fingers, stubbed it out in an ashtray. "I guess I should just skip over all the extraneous levels and head straight for the core of hell, then."

"Come hither, Dante!"

They kissed for a long time, and it was even better than it had been on the couch earlier. Paul had always thought that kissing a girl like Jenny Anderman would be terrific. But he never imagined that the longer he did it, the better it would get!

Whew! The scent of her was enough to send his brain into catatonia, and her touch sent his senses reeling.

And when he came up for air, he thought he was holding some celestial visitor rather than a mere human female who listened to Rick Springfield records.

She was so beautiful.

He felt as though he could do anything. Something like fire was running in his veins. Every sense was alive.

From the front of the house came the sound of the door opening.

"Uh-oh!" said Jenny. "Parent time."

"Right. Let's get this stuff together."

Quickly he stuffed everything into a small backpack-style book bag. Jenny meanwhile stashed the extraneous stuff like Scotch tape into a nearby drawer.

The Andermans entered.

They looked kind of like the mom and dad on *Family Ties*, faded reconstructed hippies dressed casually but expensively. Only they didn't look as good. But then nobody did. Except maybe his mom. She looked great, better than Meredith Baxter Birney any day!

Mr. Anderman had a light sweater over his vaguely paunchy form. He was carrying a paper bag.

"Oh, hi, Mom. Hi, Dad!" said Jenny.

Pleasantries were exchanged.

"This is Paul Stephens," explained Jenny. "From my science class. We were studying."

"Hello, Paul," said Mr. Anderman, shaking the very hand that had just been caressing his daughter.

"Um," Paul said, trying not to sound self-conscious. "Very pleased to meet you both."

There was an awkward moment, interrupted by Mrs. Anderman.

"Is Barnaby asleep?"

"Uh-huh," said Jenny. "Hard time getting him there, though."

A smile split Mr. Anderman's beard. "Hey!" He pulled a container from the bag. "Got some vanilla chocolate chip ice cream here. What do you say?"

"Well, actually, I promised to drive Paul home right now," said Jenny.

"Okay. Rain check, then. I gather we'll be seeing you again, then, Paul?"

"I hope so," said Paul, smiling.

"Oh, definitely," said Jenny as she pulled Paul, complete with backpack, toward the door.

"Be careful, they're predicting some flooding!" cautioned Mrs. Anderman.

"Right!" said Jenny. "I'm a good rain driver, Mom!"

Outside, heading for the Ford, Paul said, "Seem like nice people."

"Oh, they are. I have to look real hard for things to rebel against."

"Think they'd approve of this?" he asked, getting in the car.

"Approve? Oh yeah! They'd approve. But not of *my* involvement. Smart revolutionaries get other people to do the nasty work."

"Revolutionaries? With chocolate chip ice cream?"

"Hey! I hear Che Guevera was a sucker for tutti-fruitti!"

First stop, the Stephens home.

Outside it was Dr. John Mathewson's Mercedes-Benz.

"Figures. There it is!" said Paul. "German car! *Achtung, mein Führer!* Ve follow orders, *ja!* Ve make the bombs like good little Nazis, und ve eat our knockwurst und drink our beer! *Sieg belch!*"

"Yeah," said Jenny. "Hope this works."

"Oh, I've done a practice run."

"Don't sit on any sauerkraut!" She smiled adorably, and damn did she look good in her black rain slicker.

Paul got out and moved quietly up the driveway past the Mercedes. He stepped up onto the porch and peered into the window, past the curtains.

Oh, jeez.

There they were, couched cozily in the living room in front of the twenty-five-inch Hitachi. Mom was pouring wine from a new bottle. Cripes, she was drinking far too much! She was getting snookered!

Mathewson got up and put a tape in the VCR.

He went back and slipped a slimy tentacle around poor defenseless Mom, her judgment doubtlessly impaired by raw alcohol.

A title popped up on the TV. Another old movie.

Well, at least he was keeping busy for a while.

Still, his stomach churned at this awful sight. He'd get this bastard! This guy would be real sorry he ever laid eyes on Elizabeth Stephens, let alone grimy paws!

He turned and slunk back to the Mercedes, where

he got in, checked for any sauerkraut lying about, then got out the nail file Jenny had given him and violated the glove compartment once more.

He sifted through the ID cards in the billfold, handling them by the edges and wiping them off to avoid prints. There it was! He pulled out the key-card with the MedAtomics logo and Mathewson's picture and closed the glove compartment.

He ran back to Jenny's car, got in, slammed the door.

"Incredible!"

"What?" asked Jenny.

"Dr. Strangelove. He's in there, hitting on my mother! And watching my tapes too!"

"Hey, don't steam up the windshield."

"Let's go," Paul said, voice deep and firm.

"Okay. I just hope this works," Jenny said, peeling out.

"Getting cold feet?"

"No, I'm getting excited!"

"Good."

About two hundred yards short of the MedAtomics lab security area, Paul instructed Jenny to stop.

He got out and put on Jenny's rain slicker. The storm was in the air, and the branches of nearby trees were swirling about crazily. Lightning washed across the sky. It all smelled wild and chemical.

Great.

Paul went to the left front wheel of the Ford, removed the valve guard. Air whooshed as he drained the tire almost flat.

A few drops of rain splattered across the Ford's windshield. One dropped on Paul's nose. Cold.

"Right. That should do it," said Paul.

Jenny was looking fretfully down the road. "What if there's more than one guard?"

"No," Paul reassured her. "The whole place is set up so it can be watched by one person. Trust me. It's brilliant! Besides, what can they do to us? We're kids; it's a prank!"

He gave her a quick kiss, which she quite liked,

and got into the trunk, pulling the trunk down. They'd made sure it wouldn't stick and he could open it from inside.

It would be awful if he got stuck inside, Jenny mused.

With a slight shiver of excitement, she started the car and slipped it into first. She just hoped this excitement, this thrill of doing something for a good cause, would keep her going...and keep her calm through what she had to do.

As soon as she reached the security gate, she noticed the CCTV camera that Paul had mentioned. It was mounted on a post. Also, she noted a two-way intercom system.

Jenny blew her horn.

She noticed the camera panning to take her in.

Zooming and joysticking presently, doubtless. She'd been to places like this, with her father on some trips he'd taken. Kinda spooky in a cold mechanical way.

She looked around, and saw Paul peering up through the folded-down backseat.

"Hey!" she said. "Get down!"

She opened the window and leaned out.

"Hello! Anybody there? Hello?"

The guard's voice rattled from the speaker. "State your name and business, please."

"What are you? Where are you?"

"You're on a remote intercom, ma'am."

"A what?"

"Just speak into the grille. What seems to be the problem?" asked the guard.

"Uh...this isn't Baker North, is it?"

"What?"

"Baker North. Student residence? Cornell University?"

"No, ma'am. This is MedAtomics Company."

"Well," said Jenny, sounding as girlish and helpless as she could. "Where's Baker North? I've been driving around for an hour."

"Campus is on the other side of town, ma'am."

A crack of thunder, and the sky really opened up, slapping scatters of drops all over.

Jenny started to cry.

It was surprisingly easy. It almost came naturally. She sobbed with feminine gasps, leaking big glistening tears from her pretty eyes.

The camera focused, zoomed.

"Hey ... what's wrong?" asked the guard through the speaker.

"I..." Sniff. "I dunno. I'm supposed to meet my sister ... and I think something's wrong with the car and..."

"Here. Maybe I can help. I'll let you in."

The gate opened!

The wiles of a woman would do it every time, she realized, keeping the sniveling going to get her eyes nice and red, thinking about Bambi's mother and E.T. going home.

She drove through the gate and up the road to the lab buildings.

"Okay," she heard Paul say. "Now!"

She slowed the car. The trunk door opened and Paul leaped out, slammed the trunk shut, and hightailed it for the woody area between the road and the upcoming buildings.

There he goes, thought Jenny, speeding up, seeing Paul as he made his way stealthily toward where he could get around the building to the main entrance.

Good luck, you crazy, she thought.

She stopped several dozen yards from the doors.

A door opened.

The guard was coming out now, wearing a rain poncho and carrying an umbrella. The beam from a flashlight bounced as the man walked toward her car.

"Hi," he said.

"Oh, thanks so much. I don't know what's wrong!" Sniff.

"Hmm." He shined his light around the car, halting it on the afflicted wheel.

"Well, your left front wheel's flatter'n a pancake."

"Oh no!"

Snivel! Out with a Kleenex!

"Take it easy!" said the guard. "Don't cry. We'll get you fixed up. Some night. You got a spare?"

She saw Paul!

The guard's back was to the building entrance and he was sprinting to the doors. He opened the outer one to the main entrance.

"A spare what?" asked Jenny, hopelessness in her voice.

Thunder boomed ominously.

Chapter Thirteen

Paul slid the key-card through the reader, Mathewson's picture smiling the whole ride.

A red light flicked to green, and the door clicked open.

Paul hazarded a quick look back: Jenny was holding the flashlight while the fat old guard rummaged around inside. She was holding the umbrella so that it blocked the guy's sightline back to the entrance.

Good for her! he thought as he ducked inside and through the second door into the lobby. The console in the reception area was deserted. Paul moved around the desk and noted the images of the guard and Jenny on the main CRT. Nearby lay a ground plan of the building with alarm locations indicated by various legends: Corridor A, Corridor B, Clean Room, Exit A, Exit B, Area 1, Area 2. Next to this stretched a switch panel. Paul instantly recognized that it could reset the alarms when necessary. It was covered by a clear Plexi panel with a lock.

So. Now to the heart of the matter!

He ducked under the console, and there it was.

He'd glimpsed it on the way out last time he was here, and he knew it was the gate to this place. With Jenny's nail clippers as a pick, he performed his brand of mechanical magic upon the lock and opened it easily. Again using the clippers, he turned a small control marked SYNCH GEN. Adjacent were two buttons marked TAPE REWIND and TAPE ERASE. Utilizing these, he rewound and erased the taped record of the TV cameras, but left the VCR.

The effect was immediate and most gratifying.

The monitors all began to perform the familiar roll and dance of TVs on the fritz, all in crazy synch. Totally impossible to see any picture! Perfect, thought Paul, closing the access panel, and feeling adrenaline and the power of his genius sweep through him.

Uh-oh!

The front door opened.

The guard was coming through!

Keeping low, Paul dashed over to the lab corridor. Quietly as he could, he opened the door and slipped through, then peeped through the window to see what the guard was doing.

The guard grabbed a phone, dialed.

"Yes, Information?" the balding man said. "You got a number for emergency road service?"

Talking, he walked around the console and did a double take as he saw the rolling TV pictures.

"Excuse me," he said into the phone. "Call you back."

Lightning flashed and the lights quivered, and the guard looked up with a so-that's-the-problem kind of look on his face.

Perfect! thought Paul, amused to watch as the guard fiddled with the controls. The guard then picked up another phone and dialed three numbers.

"Hello? Central Office? Charlie! Fred Hawkings over at MedAtomics.... Is it raining down there?... Well, it is here. Electric storm, yeah, and it's fritzing up the whole system...."

Paul, satisfied, turned his attention back to the

corridors, A and B, running off at right angles from where he stood. Down each of these corridors, at fifteen-foot intervals, were the motion detectors, silent effective sentinels of metal and glass.

Quickly and quietly Paul rummaged through the book bag, pulling out the tin-foiled Frisbees. He held them, waiting for just the right moment. He had to time this perfectly or all was lost...He'd be found out and chucked into a detention center for the night.

"You know these damn things," the guard was saying. "Every time you get a power surge, they go crazy."

Lightning flash!

This was it!

The lights dimmed for just a flicker, and Paul seized the moment. He cocked an arm and sailed one Frisbee right down the center of the long corridor. A split second later, he did the same with the second Frisbee; one after another they flew past the motion detectors....

On the console, on the map of the corridors, little red lights popped up before the bewildered guard....

A small beeping alarm sounded.

It worked, thought Paul, and he knew it was time.

"Look at this!" said the guard. "A and B corridors just both went at once, if you can believe that! What...?"

He checked the map.

"No. Radiation checkpoint's okay. It's on its own circuit."

Leaving the book bag, Paul took off like a banshee to the other end of the corridor. Scoop up Frisbee! Run back! Grab book bag! Scoot down other corridor! Pick up second Frisbee!

Right. All of which placed him at the radiation detection unit. He sprinted through this and down the corridor that ran parallel to the main lab area. Before him was the next key-card station. Mathewson's card here proved just as useful as before. Careful not to leave fingerprints, he passed through into the throbbing, weirdly lit land of the machines.

Oh, if H. G. Wells could only see this, thought Paul as he paused a moment to catch his breath. There was the giant laser-isotope-separation unit, its small monitor/status lights shining like jewels. There was the air here of sleeping titans, snoring electricity, their stomachs grumbling from their constant diet of raw power.

A moment of awe later, Paul found himself smiling.

"Okay, fellows. Your new boss is here!"

Freddy Hawkings, night guard for MedAtomics, felt the turkey salad sandwich he'd just eaten begin to gobble in his stomach.

He held the phone in his hand, waiting for Charlie Morton to come back on the line so he could do something about this situation. Cripes, he was too old for this kind of nonsense. He had a bawling teenager outside with a flat tire and half a brain; and a goddamn thunderstorm was riding the lab like a freaking gremlin.

Gee, and he'd been looking forward to a nice quiet evening with his copies of *Penthouse* and the new Elmore Leonard novel. And he'd taken this retirement sort of job for the peace and quiet! Sheesh!

"Charlie here," came a voice over the phone. "What's the trouble, man?"

"The security console. It's going bonkers," Freddy Hawkings explained.

"Yeah?"

"So what do I do? Thing's lighting up like a video game!"

Charlie was security chief of the company assigned to guard the MedAtomics lab. "You got a big storm up there, don't you?"

"We sure do!"

"Okay, so you're getting a voltage dip, that's all," Charlie explained calmly. "Sets off the systems. Do a visual check and wait till the storm passes to reset."

"Visual check! Come on, Charlie! I don't wanna go in that lab. It gives me the creeps."

"Freddy, give me a break and do your job, okay?" He hung up.

Well, goddamn it anyway! thought Freddy. Up yours too, you jackass!

Grumpily he hung up, and made sure the alarm switches remained in the tripped position. He wasn't going to wander around this place on his bunioned feet, setting off more alarms, making more chaos.

No sirree bob, Freddy Hawkings was nobody's fool.

He took a deep breath and got ready to go.

Richard Yates had been the first to notice it.

"You do things so...quickly, Paul."

"Huh?" Paul returned.

"Whole time we've been together, I've noticed it growing. You've got this...ability. You look at something. It takes you a split second to assess it, analyze it...and snap! You make your decision! Not only that, you *act* on it. I've never seen the like."

"I guess I don't like to waste time."

Richard had shaken his mop of a head. "Uh-uh. Man, you've got something...a gift! So, anyway, could you, like, fix my Walkman for me?"

And Paul Stephens knew now that Richard was right, and Paul Stephens could feel that gift crackling in his head, zapping between his fingers as he made his way slowly toward the clean room storage-and-assay area, enclosed in a wire-mesh cage.

The truth was that it was very simple. Ideas, observations, and whatever constituted rational intuition snapped across the synapses of one's brain in nanoseconds. All you had to do was to ignore all the neurotic bullshit society had placed in you to make you think—and fear—before you act! Go with the flow. Be one with the Tao of the universe.

Paul's very favorite book in the world was something Richard had given him: *Zen and the Art of Motorcycle Maintenance* by Robert Pirsig. Pirsig had understood. You don't look at the universe or at machines as objective things built of separate parts. Everything was part of a simple process, and that process could be used with equal utility upon a broken alarm clock or a three-hundred-million-dollar Cray computer.

Inside the wire-mesh cage, a robot moved. Richard had studied such machines, which was why he'd known what it was, and what it did. Namely, determine neutron cross sections and criticality measurements by moving glass containers of varying geometries containing the plutonium-rich green gel different distances from a radiation scanner and simultaneously recording particle emission and assay data on the computer, where it could be retrieved by the scientists in the morning.

Access into the robot-assay-storage area was through a wire door complete with key-reader.

Out with Dr. John's smiling face again!

Paul kissed the picture and slipped it through the reader.

Nothing happened.

Oh-oh. He checked both sides. The reverse held two magnetic stripes, instead of the usual one. Paul turned the card upside down, then ran it through the reader again.

The gate clicked open.

Whew!

Paul entered the plutonium storage area, feeling a thrill at the sight of the ghostly stuff. In the dark, it looked phosphorescent green and slimy.

There must be enough to blow up the whole world here already.

With that sobering thought, he closed the wire-mesh door behind him and approached the robot-control computer console, glowing with a certain spectral quality itself.

On the screen of the terminal was a readout of

the functions being performed and the assay data being recorded.

Right! Time for the gloves.

He pulled out a set of Palmolive specials he'd gotten from Jenny and typed on the keyboard:

HELP

The robot arms stopped.
The CRT spewed out a response:

HELP MENU
SELECT PARAMETERS

Also, a whole laundry list of neat things this lovely piece of equipment would do, just for Paul Stephens!

Paul studied them.

Hmm. This thing was astonishingly similar to the new-model Macintosh PC he had back home.

Child's play!

Suddenly the room flooded with light.

Paul ducked under the console.

What the hell—

He peeked out, and saw that it was the guard who had just turned on the light. Doing an old-fashioned type patrol of the area. Tied around his bulky midsection was an equally bulky lead apron, chest to knees.

Jeez, thought Paul. If that guy spots me...

He hadn't thought of this... he'd figured that Jenny's good looks would keep the guard hanging around the car, not actually doing his stupid job! But then he hadn't counted on the guard being geriatric and thus with low hormone count.

Paul crouched down lower, low as he could go against the floor and the console.

Gah! It smelled of floor cleaner and shoes down here!

Speaking of shoes...

The guard's scruffy oxfords, dripping from his trip outside into the rain, halted just inches from his face.

God, he was a goner!

Worse, he'd left his book bag on a chair, in full view of the old geezer.

Arrggh!

But the old chap's full view apparently wasn't very good. Plus he seemed kind of skittish. Clearly the fellow didn't relish being in a room with all these science-fiction machines! All this green glowing gunk! All these spooky lights!

He turned tail and left, shutting off the lights behind him.

Good fellow, thought Paul, and in the newly low light he approached the computer keyboard again.

Now then, to business!

The rain drummed its steady song on the roof of the Ford.

Jenny, sitting dry if not high behind the wheel, checked her watch. She hoped to God that Paul knew what he was doing.

This was totally, *totally* crazy.

But kinda fun, too.

The thing that Jenny hated the most about this day and age was that it was so dull. She loved the stories her mom and dad used to tell about their youth. There was an excitement, a purpose, back then, in the sixties. Good music, good times...good causes.

Now...now there was something real wrong.

The kids were turning into lobotomy cases.

But not Paul Stephens. No. She could sense that this guy had something special.

About time to do my bit, she thought, reaching for the glove compartment. She pulled out her Leica, opened up the lens to its widest to catch what light there was, and snapped a photo of the front of the MedAtomics Lab for the authorities and for the article that she would eventually write for her favorite magazine in the world, *Rolling Stone*.

Jeez, her parents were going to be so *proud* of her!

Abruptly there appeared a bright light beam,

stabbing through the windows behind her. She turned, and saw a large, menacing vehicle approaching slowly. The light coned out from a side-mounted searchlight on the black vehicle.

Two-way radio chatter filtered through the rain sounds. Oh no, thought Jenny. Had Paul tripped some kind of alarm? Were these the cops?

Jenny looked closer, holding back the panic.

It was a Jeep-style all-terrain vehicle, and it looked very official.

A young man wearing a uniform stepped out. Oh, God, it was somebody like a cop....

He walked to her.

"Hi there," he said.

"Hi," said Jenny, her heart in her mouth.

"You got trouble?"

More than you'll ever know, she thought.

Okay, thought Paul Stephens. Here comes the really sticky part.

He grabbed a scintillant storage container—it looked rather like something from Mom's Tupperware collection, actually—from an open carton of the things and poured his fake gel from the shampoo bottle.

God, this stuff is as bad as Heinz ketchup, he thought, squeezing it out. Carly Simon's "Anticipation" ran through his mind.

When the last of it had finally dribbled out, he screwed the top back on and turned back to the control terminal, where he typed:

STORED MATERIAL RETRIEVAL

How easy! How fortunate they made this simple enough for most klutzy scientists to do!

He instructed the long-armed, whirring robot to execute one of its canned—that is, preprogrammed—set of commands. Namely, in this case, to pluck up one of the scintillant canisters (That's right, mister! Fresh from the cow this very dawn!)

from the rearmost rack, hustle it over and drop it...
no, better set it gently...in the air lock.

The robot made the eeriest sounds as it moved,
and the sounds echoed through the tomblike chamber like some alien monster lumbering through a
starship.

Shiver shiver!

A plutonium shake, anyone?

He grabbed the stuff from the air lock, stuck it in
a food-storage bag, sealed it and placed it in a second
bag, and sealed that too. Nasty stuff, this. Off to the
side with it, then back to the robot, who patiently
awaited this next command.

The robot obediently placed the bottle in the empty
socket, and it looked just perfect! That should hold
them for a long, long time!

Paul typed in a command for the robot to continue
the experimental procedures it was involved with
when Paul interrupted it.

He checked his watch, then skedaddled from the
area straight to the next step.

The laser!

Well, thought Freddy. Looks just fine to me. No
sign of Libyan terrorists or atomic ghosts.

He made his way outside the door of the front
entrance, and saw Terry Hicks's road service ATV,
its spotlight illuminating a fix-up job on the girl's
car.

"Yo, Freddy!" called Terry in his usual hail-fellow-
well-met macho manner.

"Hey, Terry," Freddy called back.

"Looks like rain! Whaddaya think?"

Freddy laughed at the joke and winked at the girl,
who had this tremendously relieved look on her face.
She smiled at him, a thank-you smile, and his heart
melted.

She was an awful sweet-lookin' lady.

Too sweet to stay here long with a wolf like Terry.
He'd have to keep an eye on this, that's for sure!

"Damn storm fritzed up the whole system!" he growled.

"You call it in?" Terry asked, unscrewing a lug.

"Yeah.... Tell you the truth, I'd rather have one good dog than all that fancy equipment."

All that fancy equipment, guarding all that other fancy equipment.

One of these days, it's going to get us all in real trouble, that was for sure!

Chapter Fourteen

Damn! The laser was bolted down, pointed in a direction far away from where he wanted it pointing!

Paul thought about this just a moment, before the answer occurred to him.

Or rather, he thought, he had *reflected* on the matter!

He laughed, and hopped over to the wall he knew communicated with outside. There he found a likely place.

He pulled Jenny's brother's remote-control truck from the book bag and stuck the bottle of plutonium in its fortunately accommodating bed, fastening it with a healthy amount of tape stolen from a nearby worktable.

Also lying on the table was a sharp-looking matte knife. This he grabbed and cut the insulation up to ten inches high from the ground, and pulled the stuff out, exposing the metal wall beyond.

Now...for some glasses!

He found the goggles he had used for the demo with Mathewson—or at least a pair very much like them—and put them on.

He went to the laser and he turned it on.

A few moments of warming up later, he turned on the beam . . . and the yellow-green, pencil-thin light shot out.

The tricky part was next.

Working quickly, Paul unclamped two of the special optical mirrors Mathewson had used in his demo. He sighted the laser line, calculated, then clamped the mirrors so that the beam, harmless in its present degree of intensity, reflected in a zigzag pattern, avoiding various obstacles such as support beams and machinery.

By adjusting the final mirror, he directed the beam exactly where he wanted it: through the cutout insulation.

This last mirror was the fulcrum; it was near the floor, and he could move it easily to direct the laser beam in the pattern he needed.

Hey, thought Paul. I think . . .

I think this is actually going to work!

You know, thought Jenny as she held the umbrella for the men grunting and straining with her tire, it's times like these I'm grateful for being a girl . . . and a fairly pretty girl at that! It gave her a kind of sense of power to watch these buffoons sweat and puff in the rain for her sake.

And all because she had breasts and a pretty smile and soft eyes and long silky hair and . . .

And thank heaven the guy in the truck wasn't a cop!

He apparently worked for the same company as this Fred fellow who was kneeling now in a puddle to one side of Jenny's jacked-up car.

Fred's hand slipped on the lug wrench.

"Damn!" he swore. "Goddamned Jap cars!"

"Easy, Fred," said the younger of the two, the one who doubtless had lust in his heart for her. (She could see it in his otherwise dull face.) "Haste makes waste."

He winked at Jenny, like he was some smooth Lothario or something.

Ugh.

"Yeah, well," said Freddy. "I think I'm too old for this kind of nonsense. I gotta do a check of the premises. You're the expert. You finish it."

He walked off to do an outside tour.

Jenny checked her watch.

C'mon! C'mon, Paul! You'd better hurry up and get your cute little tail outta there!

Terry gave her a smarmy smile. "Well, then, sweetie. Watch the master at work!"

The laser whined and throbbed, the sound ascending in pitch as Paul turned the knob on the remote-control device.

Paul Stephens knelt at the right angle of the beam's intersection with the optical mirror.

It sizzled through the air, just inches from his face, so close he could feel the heat! A shudder, an indescribable sense of power, passed over him. To be in control of such brilliance, such beauty!

He peaked it to steel-cutting intensity, and he could smell the burning air.

The laser sang through the darkened room, cutting a ricocheting patch, forming a crazy spiderweb pattern, ending on the wall.

Ka-pow!

The beam cut through the wall, a whisper of smoke rising up from the splatter of sparks.

Paul leaned over, careful not to stick his face into the beam (now, that would smart), and he adjusted the mirror, moving the light beam so that it continued to cut the wall, just like a welding torch on a steel plate.

The scent of scorched metal pervaded the room.

He needed a door, a tiny door . . . and he was getting it.

It was but the work of a moment.

Paul switched off the laser. Then he ran over to the new door, pulled the hot metal out with an insulated glove from the worktable, and positioned the remote-control truck.

He peeked outside.

Good. The rain had stopped. This would make things much easier.

He hit the start button of the truck and guided the thing, whirring with its little gears and batteries, through the new hole in the wall, out into the night.

Go, boy, go! Paul thought.

And with the fresh batteries he'd placed in it, it was just going to be great, all right!

Far enough!

Distant thunder sounded.

Paul stopped the truck and shut it off.

Then, using tape, he did the best he could to place the cutout piece of metal back. Hard work, all of this, but it was totally necessary. No way could he get past the radiation detectors carrying a canister full of plutonium!

Done.

He placed the insulation back, then rolled a wheeled box of equipment including oscilloscopes into place, hiding the scarred area.

Now to clean the rest of his handiwork up!

He ran back and collected the mirrors from where he had clamped them to the scaffolding and placed these just as he had found them near the laser.

Then he grabbed his bag and headed back into the corridor.

So far so good, he thought, passing through the radiation detection room, glancing at the sign.

CAUTION!
RADIATION DETECTION UNIT
MATERIALS EXCEEDING .5 M/REMS/HR WILL CAUSE
EXIT DOOR TO LOCK AND ALARM TO ANNUNCIATE

Yep, if he had carried the plutonium within even yards of this little number, every alarm in Ithaca would probably be clanging now!

Now to get out!

He sprinted down the corridor and into the reception area. Reception area: clear. Great. He scurried through and went to the glass main door, looked out, and saw Jenny's car. A young guy in a uniform was finishing up a tire change.

Jenny seemed to sense Paul's gaze, and she looked up.

Paul smiled.

He ran back to the console area, where the guard's coffee had been in the midst of preparation, and dumped a bunch of artificial creamer in it.

His little statement!

Chuckling to himself, he ran out the front door.

Jenny was looking at him like he was crazy. He held up five fingers, indicating the number of minutes he needed before rendezvous, and then he whisked around the building to retrieve the plutonium.

Five more minutes!

This jerk almost had the stupid tire on already, and Paul wanted *five more minutes!*

What was she supposed to do, jump on him and start kissing him? thought Jenny, despairing.

No way, José!

There had to be some other way, and as she looked down to the soggy ground, she immediately spotted it.

In the upended hubcap were the lugs screws that held the wheel in place.

She knelt and scooped them up and put them in her pocket.

Terry finished putting the tire in place and turned to the hubcap.

No lugs.

"Where's the lugs?" he asked, and the bewilderment on his face was truly delicious to behold.

"The what?" asked Jenny, the very picture of innocence.

"Things that hold the wheel on."

"What do they look like?" she said, batting her beautiful long lashes at him.

"Well, this means we'll be spending just a little

more time together," said the guard, who didn't seem to mind the notion at all.

Paul ran up into the cyclone fence, already estimating the exact spot where he had drilled the new door in the MedAtomics lab.

By the dim light available he searched.

He couldn't see anything!

Damn it!

And then lightning flashed, and he saw the truck, waiting patiently exactly where he had placed it.

Gotta get it out where the night lights could shed a little illumination on the matter. He turned on the remote-control device, and red lights sprang to attention.

Using the toggle switch, he guided the little truck out under the umbrella of the streetlamp-type light, letting it hum along brightly.

Now he needed to find a spot for the truck to slip through.

He searched, but had no luck.

He allowed the truck to stop while he thought about this little dilemma.

A flashlight beam angled around the building, through the faint misty air.

Oh-oh! The guard!

There were barrels of some kind directly in the middle of the concrete area. Paul directed the truck behind one.

Yikes! The guard stopped. He seemed to hear the whirring of the little electric motors!

He shot the light toward the truck, and Paul, beginning to sweat, backed up the truck into the shadow.

The guard didn't seem to be at all satisfied! He was checking out the barrels.

Sweat popped out on Paul's brow.

As the seconds ticked off in what seemed like the slowest time Paul Stephens had ever experienced, he played a crazy hide-and-seek dance with the guard, ducking back and forth through the barrels like mad, sneaking past the guard's back, once actually almost touching the guy's clunky shoe!

Finally the guard seemed satisfied.

He strode to another gate, past a culvert to drain off water, and slotted a key-card at the entrance to another—

Culvert?

That was it!

As soon as the guard's footsteps had faded away, Paul directed the truck into the opening of this culvert, then ran around to the other end of the metal drain.

Like a newly born mechanical baby, the plutonium-bearing toy truck slipped from the chute directly into Paul's hands.

"Come to papa," he said, slipping it into his book bag.

He looked up, assayed the situation, feeling totally alive.

He ran back around the building and snuck around the back of Jenny's car, where the guard, finished with his job, was busy making eyes and small talk with her.

"Oh, gee, I can't thank you enough!" Jenny was saying sweetly. She glanced at her watch. "But gosh, it's really getting late, and I really must go!"

"Okay, sweet stuff. Come round and say hey sometime, okay?"

"Yeah!" responded Jenny brightly. "I just might do that."

She got in the car, and Paul cut through the woods to meet her at the preplanned rendezvous point.

Talk about stolen goods being hot! Wow! What a coup!

He could almost feel himself being recharged by the power riding in the sack as he sprinted through the woods, then out into the glade where Jenny's car waited between the main gate and the main entrance. She opened the trunk from behind the wheel and he jumped through the hatchback door.

He slammed it shut, then moved forward, pushing

up the tilted-down backseat. "Hey, you were brilliant."

"I almost had a heart attack!"

"Don't worry," Paul assured her. "It was worth it."

They both took the time to regain some breath.

And they still had to make it out the front gate!

Freddy couldn't figure it.

He felt like something was wrong . . . not real wrong, but wrong anyway. But he couldn't find a goddamned thing on visual checks both inside and outside the labs!

Oh well, he thought, rounding the corner and noticing the taillights of the girl's car sweep around and bend toward the gate, at least we got her fixed up. He got a sense of fatherly satisfaction out of that anyway. After all, he didn't have to let her in and help her out. He could have just told her to go to hell.

But Freddy fancied himself to be a lot like John D. MacDonald's hero Travis McGee: a white knight in tarnished armor.

Terry was at the consoles, checking them out. Guy had a bit of a good touch with the stuff, so maybe he could set them right. Terry bent down and was fooling with the controls below the counter.

The pictures were still rolling as Freddy entered, but as soon as he reached the console, the kneeling guard pushed the main-synch control, and suddenly the monitors locked into place with pictures.

Good for him! thought Freddy, already feeling better as he unlocked the Plexi alarm switch panel.

He flipped the alarms back on.

The green status light went on, and everything was reset and hunky-dory once more!

With a silly grin, Terry popped up, shaking his head.

"Some cutie, huh?"

"Come on now," said Fred, picking up his cup of coffee. "You're a married man."

He watched as the car pulled up to the gate monitor. The indicator beeped.

Terry smiled up at the monitor, his hand going for the release switch.

"Man can have a little snack between meals, can't he?" He pressed. The gate swung open. The auto drove through.

"Bye, honey!" he said, waving.

Freddy took a sip of his coffee, and almost spit it out.

Damn! He'd put too much creamer in it.

"Hey, you okay?" asked Terry.

"Oh...yeah. Messed up my coffee.... Must have been when all this happened. Dumped a hell of a lot of creamer in..."

"Artificial creamer? You know, that stuff is all plastic! That stuff..." He looked around as though making sure this secret was not shared. "That stuff can kill you!"

Freddy shrugged and went to the kitchen to dump it out.

Chapter Fifteen

Jenny's foot hit the accelerator and the car shot down the road, away from the MedAtomics gate.

Paul looked back to check for headlights following.

Nothing.

Whew!

Jenny took the next curve practically on two wheels, squealing rubber.

Paul was thrown against the wall.

"Oh yeah, that's great, Jenny!" he said. "Don't attract any attention!"

He crawled into the front seat awkwardly.

The car sped down the glistening road under an enormous night sky. Clouds glided through it like galleons on a dark sea, fitfully illuminated by flashes of lightning.

Paul opened the window and let some night air splash against his overheated face.

"Okay," said Jenny, visibly calming down, but eyes still aflash with a different kind of excitement. "First thing tomorrow, we take it to Dr. Weiss—"

"Who?"

"Harry Weiss. A friend of my father's in the Chemistry Department at Cornell. He'll verify what that bottle is full of!"

"I told you what it is!"

"Yeah. But I need a second source for my article. Like Woodward and Bernstein. You know. *Washington Post. All the President's Men.*"

"Article, huh?"

"Sure. Why?"

Paul was quiet for a time.

"What's wrong with an article?"

"Nothing. You can do an article!"

"What a start to my career!"

"Let me think, though..."

"About what?"

"Gimme a second, okay?"

And Paul Stephens slumped down in his seat, watching the stunning night scenery sweep by, feeling the invigorating night air in his hair and on his face, smelling it and the sweet perfume of Jenny and her new car...

And feeling an incredible sense of power.

Thing was, he realized, it wasn't a crazy sense of power. It wasn't like he was going to dominate anyone or anything...or, goodness knows, *hurt* anyone.

But he had this chance, sitting in his backpack there...this incredible chance of making a statement in this chaotic world.

And then he felt fear...dread...

Doing this thing wasn't dangerous in itself. He was convinced of that. But if something went wrong when people found out...well, there *might* be some danger there.

Some danger, some threat.

And then he thought some more, and he thought about his dead friend Richard Yates, and a shiver ran down his spine as he remembered one of the very last things Richard had said to him when Paul had asked him why he was depressed.

"I...I feel so...so trapped, Paul. I feel like I have so much to say, to communicate...And I'm encased in quicksand. And sinking...sinking. Nobody will

listen to me! They think I'm nuts.... You think I'm
nuts, but I'm telling you, it's only a matter of time
before we're all just bits of charred skeleton in the
atomic rubble. I'd do anything...*anything* to stop it.
But what can a sixteen-year-old *do?* I can't even get
into the college where my dad is a top dog!"

"You're crazy, Richard," Paul had assured him.

But no, Richard wasn't crazy.

And Richard couldn't do anything now, but maybe
his best friend, the guy who knew him best, could
do something.

And give this world the bird at that!

The rightness of the notion infused him with purpose, and he felt the power again.

"Jenny," he said, enunciating clearly. "I had another thought..."

And he told her.

She slammed on the brakes.

"You're crazy!" she said.

"No. Now get on to my house, and I'll tell you the
rest."

At Paul's house, they immediately saw Mathewson's Mercedes still parked in the driveway.

Paul had mixed feelings about that.

They got out of the car, and Jenny's expression
was upset but thoughtful.

"Paul," she said. "All this...it's very sick!"

"I thought you wanted proof! This will be proof
...irrefutable proof!"

"But we have the stuff! Isn't that enough?"

"Enough for what?" He opened Mathewson's
Mercedes's door.

"Enough for an exposé. An article. In, like, *Rolling
Stone*, maybe. I bet they'd print it. They do a lot of
good, that's what my dad says. He's been reading it
since the good old days."

Paul was working on the glove-compartment lock.

"*Rolling Stone?* Come on, who's gonna care about
a couple of kids who stole some stuff from a lab somewhere? You want a story? Write one about a kid who
builds an atomic bomb! A real one—"

"Do you hear what you're saying?"

"Yes!"

"You are weird!"

"Oh yeah, I'm weird. I didn't make that stuff."

He took out the billfold, wiped his fingerprints off the ID card that had gotten him into MedAtomics.

"No," said Jenny. "It's too dangerous."

"But it's not! It's just a piece of equipment, like a toaster or a clock. A bunch of parts that have to be put together. So you just never put them together.... People used to be afraid of cars because they didn't understand them—"

"Cars don't kill people."

Paul stuck the ID back into the billfold and placed it back into the glove compartment.

"Cars have killed more people than all the atomic bombs in the history of the world."

"That's not a logical argument!" Jenny snapped.

"I'm not talking about logic. I'm talking about..." He shut the door of the Mercedes, then smiled up at Jenny. "The first privately built nuclear device in the history of the world!"

Jenny started back for her car.

Paul followed her, wondering what to do. He needed her help for this little business, there was absolutely no question about that! She could spill the beans, she could say no, she could do a lot of different things that would mess this idea all up.

"Jenny," he said. "This is your chance...our chance...to make a difference."

She stopped at the car, back still stiff, facing him.

He chanced a hand on her shoulder, and he could feel that shoulder relax under his touch.

She turned to him, and the answer was in her eyes.

She fell into his arms and kissed him like he had never been kissed before, and it was incredible.

Her eyes shone with purpose and with something more as she broke away for some breath.

"Well," she said, moving provocatively in his embrace. "Thank you for a very interesting evening!"

Chapter Sixteen

Mr. Wilke squinted down at the piece of paper, reading.

Paul waited for the response to his application here in the corridor of Ithaca High School, outside chem lab. He'd been a model student all day, just in preparation, and now he was hitting up on old Wilke.

"Science fair?" said the guy, looking up doubtfully. "Really?"

"Uh-huh!" Paul said, smiling eagerly. "The Forty-fifth Annual National Talent Search ... you get to go to New York ..."

Wilke scratched his head and then nodded. "Oh yeah. The same one Roland's entering, huh?"

He checked out the back, where Paul's description of his project was penned.

"'Retinal deprivation and auditory enhancement in the common cricetus.' Zoology?"

"Uh-huh. I'm going to raise a generation of hamsters in the dark and see if it improves their hearing."

"Paul, that's a kind of weird experiment, isn't it?"

"No, no," insisted Paul. "I think the field's wide open. I think I have a chance to win."

Wilke shrugged. "Well then, go for it." He winked at Paul. "Learned that phrase on TV last night."

"Gee, Mr. Wilke, you're so...hip!"

Mr. Wilke grinned. "Yeah, well, it's great to see someone turn over a new leaf."

He handed the form back to Paul, then walked back into the classroom.

As Paul made sure old Wilke had put his X in the right place, Jenny came up to him, holding two packed bag lunches.

"Well?"

"Well, he bought it." Paul held up the signed form.

"Good." She held up the lunches. "How about a little caviar, Brie, and vino?"

"And thou?"

"Would you settle for salami and cheese?"

"Well, I *am* hungry."

"You're terrible. Let's go outside. It's nice."

"Okay."

Outside, they took up residence under a tree and they had lunch.

"Just how do you build an atomic bomb, Paul?" asked Jenny casually, in the way of conversation.

"Very carefully."

She laughed and he sipped his milk thoughtfully.

"Seriously. I really didn't follow that section in chem lab."

"Test's next week, might as well give you a crash course. Wilke's making it seem much too hard, throwing in all kinds of weird extra stuff about quantum physics and everything."

"Yeah."

"Okay. Well, that stuff we swiped?"

"Plutonium!"

"Plutonium 239, to be exact. Uranium got Hiroshima, plutonium got Nagasaki. You notice on the element chart how far up they are?"

"Yeah. Not like simple stuff like hydrogen and oxygen."

"Exactly. That's because they're made of lots of protons and electrons and neutrons, and anything much higher than uranium is so complex that it's very unstable...that is, all those atomic materials fall apart easily."

"Short half-lives!"

"Yes, and since all the original material forged in the beginning of the universe is billions of years old now...well, the higher elements are either gone or very rare. These are called transuranics."

"Because they're past uranium?"

"Hey, see! It all makes sense. Anyway, plutonium was the first man-made element produced in sufficient amount to see. As I recall, it was created in 1940 at the University of California at Berkeley."

"So uranium and plutonium...they're just elements. What gives them that old Kiloton Kick?"

Paul took a bite of his sandwich and chewed around the words. "Like I say, they're unstable. The atomic forces that hold them together...well, that's just a simple way of saying it, but it will have to do...are comparatively easy to knock apart."

"You mean, like an elaborately built Tinkertoy my brother attacks?"

"Yeah. But the thing is, what you don't see with a Tinkertoy construction is the tremendous amount of energy released when it comes apart."

"Yeah, you mean, MC squared is equal to E?"

"By George, she's got it. In fact, Jenny, if you knock apart these plutonium Tinkertoys right, so much energy is unlocked that this energy starts knocking apart lots of other, more stable elements around it, creating a tremendous explosion."

Understanding crossed Jenny's face. "A chain reaction!"

"That's right. That's essentially it."

"Okay, but don't you, like, need about a zillion sticks of dynamite to knock over even a plutonium Tinkertoy?"

"Not anymore. There's lots more sophisticated explosives these days than dynamite....That's not all, though. It's all got to be put in the right kind of container and stuff, and the explosives have got to be shaped right....And then there's the triggering mechanism....It can all be done...I just have to figure it all out!"

"I don't know, Paul....It sounds pretty hard. I mean, it took years to figure out how to make this kind of bomb back in the forties and fifties...."

"Yes, but the most casual of technology now is far advanced from the most sophisticated technology then. I just have to use my head, and all those research books available...all in the library at Cornell ...plus a few concentrated ones I got from Richard Yates, my atomic pal."

Jenny took a few thoughtful sips from her carton of milk. "Yeah, but what's going to prevent it all from going off in your face?"

"It's not like chemistry class, Jenny. It's very hard to make plutonium fission. You have to do it just right...."

"But the explosives, Paul. The explosives!" She touched his arm, and there was concern and caring in her soft blue eyes.

"Like I say, real safe. Plastic explosives!"

"But, Paul, where are you going to get plastic explosives?"

"Hey, where was I going to get plutonium?"

"Oh. Yeah. You are pretty inventive. And just plain pretty too, come to think of it."

"You're not so bad yourself."

He leaned over and gave her a kiss.

"Hmm. You're getting close," she said.

"Something wrong with me? I mean, I'm only sixteen. I've got to practice at this kind of stuff! You know, kissing manuals, hugging manuals...I've got 'em all and I'm studying hard, I promise."

She laughed, and the sound of it in the sunshine, amid the smell of the trees and the grass and the Lebanon bologna sandwich, was delightful.

"No, you ninny. The kissing's just fine." She leaned

over and they did it again. "You're getting close, all right ... close to critical mass!"

"Hey, I didn't teach you that term! You been kissing some other teenage genius?"

"No," she said softly. "Only you, silly. Only you."

Chapter Seventeen

"Here we go," said Mr. Adams, the school's head custodian, unlocking the door. "Hope this will do."

It was a workshop, one of many from the age of real Ithaca High School industry, when students were students, seriously bent on scholarship and hard experimentation, and endeavored mightily to further Knowledge for Its Own Sake. It had only recently been used in any real way in the past few years, but this time it was being used for Knowledge for Hard Cold Cash.

"Thanks, Mr. Adams," said Paul, allowing Jenny to go in first. "This will do just fine."

And for Paul Stephens, this place would be used for Knowledge for the Joke of the Century!

"Whew!" said Jenny. "Smells awful!"

"Hamsters won't care," said the evening custodian, lifting his cap and scratching his white-haired head thoughtfully. "Now, remember, I got to lock up by ten every night. Otherwise, Paul, it's all yours, and I won't bother you if you don't bother me!"

"Sure, Mr. Adams."

"Could you leave the door open?" Jenny asked.

Paul ignored the smell—just age, must, and stale

turpentine, nothing serious—and put his notebook down on the scarred wooden worktable. He turned on the lamp above this table and opened the book and took out a Flair pen.

"So, you were going to tell me exactly how you intend to do this," said Jenny.

"You're going to have to close the door, then."

Jenny thought about this a moment. "Okay," she decided.

"All right," said Paul, when she came back. "Here's the outline and flowchart of the procedure I'm going to have to use to build this thing."

He wrote down: 1) design.

"First, I got to do some serious studying on the actual way this has got to fit together. This is going to be the hardest part. It's the theoretical part."

"But, Paul, you're only a high school student! You act like you're a doctor in engineering or something."

"You forget, Jenny, that this is the Age of Information. You don't have to understand a gourmet-cooked meal to eat it and derive nutrition. You just have to find the meal, and know how to stick it in your mouth. Everything else is natural....I have just enough knowledge to know where to research ...and enough knowledge and ability to understand what they are saying in these books and papers.... The rest is just trial and error, which I can do much faster than Edison, on a computer, 'cause I'm dealing with geometry and equations and stuff."

"I don't know, Paul."

"Look. It's real simple. When Newton discovered much of what we call modern physics way back in the seventeenth century, he said it all. 'I can see things because I stand on the shoulders of giants.'"

"You mean, he was using the work of a lot of other scientists."

"Exactly. You see, most people just don't get this: they think life's a solo kind of thing. You got to prove yourself. You got to start from scratch, like Horatio Alger or something. Bullshit. All you have to do is to fill in a few gaps between the huge amount of knowledge available. Geniuses are simply people who use all available data and structure their observations on that data in a logical fashion."

"People who see patterns..."

"Precisely.... And those 'patterns' are theories. The whole atomic theory is marvelously elegant and simple... and it works. Now quantam physicists are still finding out *Twilight Zone* stuff about what goes on on the subatomic level.... But no matter what that means, when you stick your key in the car, you can be pretty sure it's going to start, and when you drop an A-bomb, you can also be sure it's going to make a huge explosion."

"Well, good luck," said Jenny doubtfully.

"Yeah," said Paul, starting to write again. "This part is next."

He wrote: 2) electronics.

"That's easy," said Jenny. "Soldering and wires and stuff."

"Right. And all the equipment I need is readily available.

He wrote: 3) implosion trigger.

"Tricky part," said Paul. "But this guy I met, guy who went out with my mom, is an explosives expert. I'll give him a call, maybe he can help me out."

"Explosives, Paul?" said Jenny.

"Yeah, like I told you before, you need a shaped explosion to set off the chain reaction."

"I still don't understand."

"Look. I'll draw it out for you."

He wrote down: 4) core. "I guess you know what that is."

"I should. I helped you steal it."

"Yeah. So, at the center of our bomb we have something called an initiator. Ball of metal. The plutonium is around this ball of metal, and covering that is a three-inch reflector shield... beryllium, I believe. Now, we need the shaped explosions in a symmetry around this shield, and this is the big secret of the atom bomb, Jenny." He drew a quick picture. "'Cause, you know, when the bombs at Hiroshima and Nagasaki went off, they were so primitive that only a part of their cores was properly fissioned."

"Wow!"

"Yeah. I read all this in John McPhee's *Curve of Binding Energy* years ago.... But I just read it again last night, so that's why I sound so glib." He gave her a silly smile, and she hit him in the arm. "Anyway," he continued, "like I say, this is the great secret of the atom bomb. That's what McPhee talks about in his book.... This guy, Theodore B. Taylor, was kind of half physicist and half inventor, and he worked some of the best designs for the proper shaping of the explosives. They're like lenses, you see, and what you want to set off is an imploding shock wave, spherical..."

"And then, fusion!"

"No, Jenny. Fission."

"Chain reaction!"

"That's right. What we talked about."

"Simple!"

"If it was that simple, though, lots more people could make it...."

"But you just said—"

"We have a couple of problems. First, making the plutonium. Second, surviving it...."

"What? You mean, radiation?"

"No...we've highly sophisticated measures for that. No, you see, because of its highly unstable nature, plutonium is very poisonous. As a matter of fact, I bet there are a lot of dead terrorists out there, people who tried to make a bomb and fooled with plutonium. You don't fool with plutonium."

Jenny's eyes got huge. "But...but...we did!"

"But, Jenny, we're not stupid fanatical terrorists! I know the precautions. I know where to get the equipment to work with it! And anyway, I'm a genius!"

"I'm glad you think so!"

"So now"—he tapped the paper emphatically—"I begin. But, Jenny," he said, frowning, getting serious, "I must request one thing in the way of aid."

"I'm not going to touch that plutonium, I can tell you that."

"No. Not the plutonium. Me." He grinned. "A working scientist needs much love to inspire him. Hugs and kisses, stuff like that."

He grabbed her, and she melted into him reluctantly.

"Good thing," she said, after a soft kiss, "I happen to be turned on by mad scientists."

Paul Stephens sat in his workshop, alone, with his partly assembled bomb and a half-eaten Mars bar.

Jenny had left a half hour ago, to do her homework, but Paul was still intent on finishing this part of the project.

He gobbled down the last of the chocolate and almonds and air, and tossed the wrapper behind him to lie with all the other wrappers strewn on the floor. Then he set back to work with his soldering iron and solder.

HOW TO MAKE AN ATOMIC BOMB
TAKE THESE ELEMENTS:
Circuit boards and assorted computer parts
One VW key, with ignition lock
Photo-strobe units
Batteries
Mounting boards and connectors
Electrical wires, screws, lugs
One toolbox
One vise
Digital clock
Computer circuit cards
ADD PLUTONIUM CORE.
MIX VERY CAREFULLY.
DON'T DROP!

Paul Stephens worked hard and efficiently at his task. His father was the one who had taught him to do this kind of work—from the age of seven or eight, he'd been working with circuit boards and electrical connectors, making all manner of Heath-kits at first, and then progressing to his own contraptions. It took a certain knack to be able to do this sort of thing—a knack, plus a good deal of dexterity and patience.

Paul was a whiz at it, and he could have gone faster...but he took his time, making sure everything was right, testing the current flow in all the connectors when he had soldered them in. After all, this baby was going to be extremely well scrutinized, once he won the prize. There would be all kinds of papers written about it, and suppose there was an article in *Omni* about it, which mentioned a faulty placement of a resistor...

He'd just die of embarrassment!

He was getting there, no question about it. It had taken him a couple of weeks to actually design the thing: weeks of intense research and diagramming. However, the research had borne much fruit, as he expected it would. The real trick would be in shaping the charge. Spies in the fifties had been executed for giving this secret to the Russians. How could an eighties kid come up with it?

But he would, somehow, he knew it. The thing about a project like this was to keep on going, paint yourself into a corner, then figure out the solution once you've done that. Often as not, the subconscious somehow *knew* the answer; it was merely a matter of figuring it out, once you were in the corner.

The gadget was taking shape. It was time to test the timer.

The thing had three key positions. OFF, ON/SET, and COUNTING.

The digital readout had three digits in the hour position, two in minutes, two in seconds.

Now it read: 000:00:00.

Paul set it for ten seconds, then turned it on.

It counted down.

At 0, the strobe units all fired at once.

Paul smiled and continued working.

Close to closing time, he took the Flair and one

by one he crossed out the first three aspects of the project.

All that was left was the core.

The hardest part of all.

Chapter Eighteen

Paul Stephens's teammates scurried about on the soccer field like crazy people, vying for a good kick at the tumbling ball.

Paul didn't care much for gym class. But he had to admit, he was pretty good at some participatory sports, like this one, and so far his soccer team was doing well in the occasional intraclass games held after school.

Still, even now, he wasn't paying much attention to his teammates kicking and grunting.

No, he was thinking about his project.

Shaped charge. Implosion.

But how?

The mathematics were... well, they were just beyond belief. He needed a goddamn Cray, not a puny Macintosh, to figure this baby out.

No wonder it was such a secret! There had to be just the right distribution of explosive, patterned in just the right geometrical array, set to detonate at the precise same moment.

But what was that pattern? What was that array?

"Hey, Stephens!" cried a voice. "Heads up!"

Wha—

Bam!

The soccer ball slammed right into his head, bouncing away into the waiting knees of a defender, who immediately kicked it out of the danger zone!

"Good save, Stephens!" cried a teammate.

Paul almost fell flat on his butt.

He staggered around for a good five seconds before he recovered, and when he did feel firmly planted, albeit with a big headache, he happened to look up in time to see the soccer ball sailing toward him, closer, closer... larger, larger...

And his headache was forgotten.

The geometrical formation!

It had to be something like a soccer ball!

The ball landed directly in front of an opposing team member, who immediately kicked it past Paul, and into the net behind him.

"Hey, where are you, Stephens?" someone cried. "Mars?"

"No," said Paul. "Pluto."

The watch said 11:45.

The guy had said he'd show up at 11:30.

Paul sat in the pile of dirt in the vacant lot on Saturday morning, waiting, uneasy.

He needed this stuff, and he was counting on this delivery, and if he didn't get it today, there was no way he'd get the right stuff to get the project ready for the fair.

11:46.

The construction guy had been very helpful, doubtless hoping he could get another date with his mother. Science paper? Information? Explosives? Sure. What you need to know, pal?

He'd needed to know the most powerful plastic— i.e., shapable—explosive around.

The guy told him, but he didn't have any samples, though he knew that the local army base kept it, and he had a contact whom he used to get it, when he needed extra-special stuff to blow something up.

Just for research, Paul assured him, could he have the number?

Sure can. Say, how's that pretty mom of yours?...

Well...So he'd called, he'd made the deal with the guy...code name Dembo, Army Surplus...

And now...

An old battered car suddenly pulled off the road. A young guy in army fatigues behind the wheel hailed him, then pulled up his car beside the dirt pile.

"You Stephens?" asked the guy, maybe nineteen, twenty years old.

"Yeah. Got the stuff?"

"Sure do, if you got the bread!" A broad smile below the crew cut made him look totally ludicrous.

"Sure do."

The guy opened his car's trunk and pulled out packages of stuff with army stenciling, each about the size of two-quart milk cartons.

"Okay. C-4. High explosive," said Dembo. "Fantastic stuff. Very stable. You can burn it, you can drop it, you can hit it with a hammer—but don't be around when it goes off. Hey, Paulie, what're you gonna do with this? *No,* don't tell me."

"Science project," Paul explained, hauling the stuff toward his bike.

"Right. Whatever. Need anything else? Ammo? C rations? Hand grenades? Toilet paper?"

"No," said Paul, returning to Dembo. "This is great. How much?"

"Make it sixty..."

Paul paid him. "You seem to enjoy your position in the army."

"Oh yes, it's a living. Take care, genius. Don't blow yourself up, okay?"

"I know what I'm doing," said Paul.

"Cantaloupes!" said Jenny, staring at Paul's handiwork.

"That's right. I used a bunch to cut up and figure out how to put this baby together. So now I've got the design, and here it is."

It was partly completed, with a hole large enough to fit the core through. It was the primary detonator assembly—hexagons and pentagons of shaped explosives, looking less a soccer ball now than a honeycomb made by large, demented bees.

"Uh...right..." said Jenny. "So what's next?"

Paul pointed to the box that had just been delivered to him, special order.

"It's called an isolette, Jenny. It's an infant incubator. I'm going to hook it up with a filter system and use gloves to work with the plutonium."

"But you said it's poisonous..."

"I'll also be wearing a respirator."

"And I'll be wearing a hair dryer, on the other side of town!"

"Good idea," said Paul, nodding his head seriously.

"Paul, really...if anything happens to you..." She touched him tentatively.

"Look, I know what I'm doing, I told you."

"Okay. But be careful."

She kissed him.

He removed the bottle of plutonium and gel, and with a care and patience that truly taxed his innermost resources, he opened the cap and poured the contents of the bottle into a flask, through a filter funnel.

If it weren't for all these precautions, Paul Stephens thought, I'd be a dead teenager now.

He added some liquid, stirred it with a glass rod, and the remaining green gel dissolved away, running through the funnel and leaving dull silvery flakes of plutonium.

There it is, he thought. There it is.

The rest was simple.

At the school shop, he fashioned the central metal core, the initiator, from aluminum on the lathe. For the reflector, he utilized salad bowls.

Working with the isolette, he fashioned the core

of his device...this was the bit that was really going to wow the world. The skill, the care, the genius...

Ah yes...

And it was almost complete.

Chapter Nineteen

It was finished.

Paul put the cat box on the workbench and lifted off the top to show Jenny.

He had altered the wooden box, complete with handle and airholes, to contain his spanking-new gadget, with a special protected section for the core.

Jenny blinked.

"That's it?"

She was wearing a soft cashmere sweater, and she looked lovely, but Paul barely noticed, his machine obsession cranking now in full gear.

"What did you expect?"

"I dunno. It looks so simple."

Paul had to think about that for a moment, think about the right response. He shouldn't yell at her. ...How could she know?...He mustn't get so wound up in techno-fever, even though it rode him now like the Old Man of the Sea.

"All great designs are simple. The safety pin. The zipper. The nuke..."

He took the plutonium core from its special compartment in the case and held it out to Jenny.

"What's that?" she asked.

"The core. The stuff. Plutonium. Go ahead, it won't hurt you."

She looked at it as though she were Supergirl and it was kryptonite. "Uh-uh."

Paul said, "I mean not the way it is now.... The outside is aluminum and it's sealed in about ten coats of epoxy."

Tentatively she held it in her palm.

She gave it back very quickly.

"It's warm," she said.

"Body temperature, almost. From alpha emission."

"From what?"

"Nothing. It's okay. See, it goes in the middle here, it's surrounded by the C-4—"

Jenny got a funny look on her face.

"Paul, let's give it back," she said as he replaced the shiny sphere.

Paul could barely believe his ears.

"What?"

"It's too scary," Jenny insisted.

"It's not scary," he said, looking at her with disbelief. "I'm totally in control here. Why is it scary?"

Jenny said, "I mean, what if it went off? I mean, Paul, it's a bomb, Paul. That's what bombs *do!*"

Paul was bewildered. "How can it go off?"

"I dunno. I'm not a scientist."

Paul sighed. "Look. You have to know how to put it together. You have to put the batteries in and make lots of connections and put the core in and set the timer, and I'm the only one who knows how to do it, okay?"

"Yeah, but what if it just went off?"

"But it can't!"

"Three Mile Island wasn't supposed to go off! Planes aren't supposed to crash! But they do!"

"You're being irrational," Paul insisted.

"So humor me."

"Okay, you want to know, if somebody put it all together, and set the timer, and it just went off somehow, which is totally impossible."

"Uh-huh."

"Well, if all that happens, and it works...you get a fireball."

Jenny's eyes grew wide.

"What do you mean, a fireball?"

"Fifty million degrees, a hundred yards across, hotter than the sun. Everything between here and maybe the athletic field gets vaporized."

Jenny's face got ashen. She looked wobbly. She grabbed the worktable for support and sat on a chair.

Paul went to her.

"Come on, relax. I know what I'm doing. I took a million precautions. Remember how you said how nobody does anything? Well, we're doing something! I mean...imagine the effect when we unveil it at the fair—"

"The effect on who?"

"Everybody. That lab. The newspapers. The whole world. It'll be incredible!"

"Paul, are you doing this for the world or for your ego?"

Paul thought about that, and looked at her.

"I guess I'm doing it because I *can* do it."

"You're enjoying this."

"Yeah. Yeah. So?"

"Paul, what's happening to you?"

"Jenny, I'm no mad scientist! I'm not going to blow anybody up! This is all a lark, yeah, and it's fun, yeah, but ultimately...ultimately it will help. I really believe that, or I wouldn't be doing it. Please believe me!"

"Okay. I guess so. I just got a little scared."

"Jenny, don't freak out on me. I need you...I need your...your support here. I could not have done any of it without you."

Jenny looked thoughtful. "Yeah. I guess you're right. I guess I'm kind of neck-deep in it."

"You bet."

"Okay. It is...well, we'll show it at the science project and I'll write my article, and that's it, Paul!

I'm not going to date any guy whose *main* passion is making atomic bombs!"

"Great, Jenny."

"Look, I gotta run an errand. You going to be okay in here?"

"I think so."

"Let me leave you something to remember me by."

She held him and kissed him, and for a moment he forgot about bombs.

But only for a moment.

When she was gone, Paul took out the sections of his homemade A-bomb and placed them on the table before him.

He stared at them a moment.

He started to put them back, but then was hit by a strange compulsion.

Hey. Why not?

Carefully he began assembling the components, a faraway look in his eyes.

When everything had been set into place, he turned a key one click and set the timer for ten seconds.

00:00:10, it read.

Wow. He could feel the machine fever coming over him, this intellectual frenzy. He felt like Zeus himself, putting together a lightning bolt.

He had to feel the pulse of it, the throb, the power!

Starting to sweat a little, he put the plutonium core in the device, placing the plug in afterward.

He screwed the sections together.

Yes. Right. Ready for activation.

Paul Stephens touched the key with his fingers. He placed the slightest pressure on it, just to feel what it was like...

This must be what it was like to sit in one of those Minutemen missile silos, he thought. This must be what it's like to be President of the United States, or the Commissar of the Soviet Union....

The hard cold metal of the key to eternity pressed into the fleshy part of his fingers.

BAM!

Paul's finger jumped away from the key.

Paul himself jumped about two feet in the air.
BAM BAM BAM BAM! continued the sound.

Somebody was knocking at the door, that was all.

"Just a minute!" Paul called, and he quickly disassembled the mechanism, thinking he *never* wanted to be President or Commissar. He placed a dropcloth over the project; then he went to the door of the workshop and unlatched it.

It was the custodian, his eyes dull and unsuspicious. "Closing up, young fella."

Paul said, "Oh, right—thanks!"

He went back and packed everything up, smiling to himself but still feeling a bit spooked.

What an accomplishment!

But still there was a chance to back down from going all the way. Maybe Jenny was right. Maybe he should just turn the plutonium in, then show them what he had done. Maybe that would be enough to let these particular authorities realize the error of their ways.

Maybe he should forget about going to New York. Maybe he should forgo the thrill of setting up a working A-bomb at the National Science Fair.

Maybe ... perhaps ...

Perhaps he should sacrifice the excitement of the flashing bulbs of the press, the awe of his fellow students, worldwide coverage....

Perhaps he should forget about the thrill of winning the first-place prize at the fair, beating hell out of Roland....

Naw, he thought, and smiling broadly he packed up his own personal Manhattan Project into its cat box and he headed home.

Chapter Twenty

As Paul Stephens lugged his cat box and its hot contents home to Mother, milk, and cookies, a technician named Peter Flannagan was showing something of importance to Ed Wilson, radioactive materials control officer for MedAtomics, in his office.

"Lot thirty-seven," said Flannagan. "Completely flat."

He had just placed a large piece of graph paper in front of Wilson, a balding, portly, convivial sort, who immediately lost his usual pleasant attitude.

"Did you recheck it?" asked Wilson.

"Oh, sure. Three times."

Wilson nodded. "Run a full-spec analysis, and keep this between us."

"Right," said Flannagan. "I'll do it in the morning."

"No, you won't. Do it tonight. I'll need the results in the morning."

Flannagan did not quibble. This was indeed something of great seriousness.

* * *

For Paul's part, however, somehow he'd lost much of his own nervousness. Once more this trip to New York was a lark, and everything would turn out according to plan. He'd built the thing, hadn't he? He had done the hard part already.

Everything else would be gravy.

That night, he watched TV awhile, then went up to his bedroom and played one of the albums Richard had convinced him to buy, a solo album by Dave Pegg, who was prime mover in the current version of Fairport Convention, and concurrently the bassist for Jethro Tull. It was called *The Cocktail Cowboy,* and Paul sipped half of a Bass ale to help him go to sleep as he listened to it.

Everything was set to go, everything was geared up.

He just wished that Richard Yates were still around to see it all.

To the sound of mandolins, Paul Stephens read the new copy of *StarDate* magazine, and then he slept like a baby.

In the morning, his mother fussed over him like some kind of hen or something, and it annoyed him terribly.

"Did you eat your vitamins?" she wanted to know.

"Yeah, Mom," he said, zipping up his overnight bag.

Outside, dawn had just come up and the day was looking a bit blowsy.

"New York!" she said, shaking her head at the very thought. "My Paul is going to New York City by himself. God, you're almost an adult now!"

"New York, New York—the city that never sleeps ...and looks like hell in the morning," said Paul, copping an opening line from the David Letterman show.

There came the sound of a car outside, pulling up in the driveway.

"That'll be Jenny," said Paul, putting on his sport coat, then hoisting up his overnight bag and his cat box with its surprise filling. "Thanks for breakfast, Mom."

She followed him outside to where the car waited, purring in the dewy freshness of the morning.

"Now, Paul, New York is not a safe city. Keep your money in your front pocket, you hear?"

"Mom," said Paul, stowing his luggage in the hatchback. "It's only New York, not Calcutta."

"Good luck, sweetheart!" she said, waving them off as Paul got into the car. "Good-bye, Jenny!"

Jenny began backing out of the driveway after a wave. "So long."

"And call when you get there!"

Jenny bid adieu with a double beep of her horn.

"Your mom's pretty neat," said Jenny, driving down the highway, the sun a little higher in the sky. "Not every American mother would let her son drive off to a hotel in Sin City with a sexy girl."

"Yeah, well, she's probably glad to see me go, so she and Albert Einstein can make love on the dining-room table or something."

"Paul! Don't... I mean, she's your mother!"

"Sorry, I don't like apple pie, either. No, Jen, I've got no illusions how I got here, and I know for sure the processes are still working there." He shrugged. "I just kinda wish my dad hadn't... well... never mind."

Jenny had met Dr. Mathewson the previous week and she had to say something. "Paul, come on now. John's a really great guy."

"A really great guy who makes plutonium for bombs that might blow up the world."

"Hey, Guy Fawkes! You've just made a bomb yourself, remember."

"I'm not going to blow anybody up with it—"

"Get off it, Paul! You know you like John Mathewson... you're just like two peas in a pod."

"Yuk!" Paul said, knowing it was true but unwilling to admit it.

Meanwhile, Dr. John Mathewson was dealing with a matter entirely different at the MedAtomics lab.

Flannagan the technician, Mathewson the scientist, and Wilson the supervisor were reading the requested report on the contents of the suspect canister, which sat nearby.

Peter Flannagan read the report out loud.

"Water, citric acid, sodium laureth sulfate, hydrolyzed animal protein, glycerin, U.S. FDS coloring number five—"

Mathewson was stumped and was beginning to fluster. "What the hell is it?"

Peter Flannagan looked up from the report. "Shampoo?"

"Shampoo?" returned John, disbelief plain in his voice.

Flannagan continued reading. "We think either a generic local brand or something called Alberto's VO Five. Oh yeah, and some glitter."

"Glitter?"

"Shredded aluminum foil. Like on greeting cards."

Wilson said, "Thank you, Peter. You may go."

Wilson handed Mathewson the printout.

"I guess somebody has a weird sense of humor," suggested Mathewson in a lame attempt to get some time to think.

Wilson said, "I checked this one out, John. The time key record has you in the building four weeks ago, Sunday night, at... 11:08 P.M., out at 11:49."

He handed him another sheet of paper.

"No," said Mathewson. "This is a mistake."

"You weren't here?"

"No." Mathewson's mind was racing hard.

"Well, somebody was. With your card."

"No," Mathewson insisted. "That's impossible."

Wilson shrugged and tapped the paper. "Hard data there, man."

"Ed, it's a computer. It's not infallable..." Mathewson knew damned well where he'd been that night. At Elizabeth's....It was a most memorable night, with the wine, the kisses, the sound of thunder...."Wait a minute...wasn't that the night of that big electrical storm?"

"I don't know. So what?"

"But there's your answer! There was a power drop-out and you got a little garbage in the system."

Wilson reconsulted the printout.

"But it says right here, Mathewson, 11:08."

"I know, I know . . . but do me a favor. Check the system, okay? And give it a few days. You know these guys . . . cabin fever. It's a joke, I'm sure. It will turn up."

"It's a significant amount. I have to report it."

"Come on," said Mathewson, feeling a little desperate, a little nagging thought at the back of his mind. "They'll be all over us. I'm on a crash program here. You want to bring everything to a dead stop just because of a little glitch?"

"I'm sorry, John. I don't make the rules."

Wilson strode away, and Mathewson almost ran to his office to check out that little nagging thought.

His finger shook a little bit as he dialed the number.

"C'mon, Elizabeth," he whispered tersely. "Be there!"

She answered.

"Hi."

"Oh, hi, John. . . . What do I owe this unusual pleasure to?"

"Could I, uh . . . could I speak to Paul?"

"Paul's away until tomorrow night."

"Oh. . . . Where?"

"New York. He has a project in the science fair. He didn't tell you?"

"What kind of project?" Mathewson said, his stomach sinking.

"Something at school. Guinea pigs, I think. No— hamsters. Can I leave a message?"

"No . . ." Backpedaling time! "I just had some tickets to the ball game . . . Oh gosh."

"What?"

"They need me on the floor. Usual dumb crisis. . . . Oh, yeah, what hotel is he staying at?"

"The New York Penta."

"Great. Maybe I'll give him a ring, okay?"

"Sure."

"Great. Well, I better go. Bye."

"Bye." Her voice sounded mildly puzzled, and Mathewson couldn't blame her.

God help him, it couldn't be...

But he was going to have to check it out anyway.

He got his jacket and headed out.

The local FBI agents had gotten there before he did.

As he pulled up he noted the white sedan and white van nearby, both with MedAtomics logo and legend: detection units from the lab.

He'd confided in Wilson his fears; and Wilson's first reaction had been to hit the red alert, call up everybody.

Mathewson didn't really blame him.

This was deadly serious.

The FBI agents, plain-brown-wrapper faces in plain-gray-wrapper suits, were interviewing a baffled-looking high school student.

"And what is your name again?" asked one as John got out and slammed the door behind him.

"Max Perkins," said the kid, wide-eyed.

"And you knew that Paul Stephens was inside here, working on a project?"

"Oh... yeah.... He needed the area for his science project. That's what he told everyone, and that's what he got."

"But you never actually went inside and saw what he was doing."

"No," said the dark-haired kid.

"Why not?"

"He never asked me. What's the problem? Was he sexually abusing the hamsters or something?"

Wilson chose that moment to arrive.

"Okay," said John. "This was where he was working.... We'll know for sure in a moment."

"Oh yeah, you'll know," said an FBI agent, shaking his head. "You should see the stuff in there!"

"Let's do," said Wilson, signaling Mathewson to follow him.

Inside the workshop, MedAtomics technicians wearing eerie white protective suits and masks were searching the place. Already Mathewson could see that they had found a candy-bar wrapper: a pair of gloved hands were gingerly holding it a moment. It was dropped into a plastic bag. The other guy was holding a Geiger counter near a school globe about a foot in diameter.

He opened it, and it split into halves at the equator.

Snuggled inside were templates: a pentagon and a hexagon.

Mathewson recognized them as templates for shaped charges of plastic explosives.

Jesus! thought Mathewson.

And what was that?

An address label on a box: RUSH! LOS ALAMOS NATIONAL LABORATORIES—ATTENTION: RADIOACTIVE WASTE DISPOSAL DIVISION—USE EXTREME CARE! DO NOT OPEN.

It was a carton that had contained an isolette/glove box that Paul would have had to use to deal with the plutonium. The carton was sealed with a great deal of tape.

"Take a look at this, sir," said one of the white-suited men.

Mathewson accepted the rolled-up length of paper and unscrolled it. Drafting paper. Blue drafting paper and...

And spread upon it was a design...

The design.

There'd been a lot of erasures and a lot of redrafting, and the final product was not precisely the present-day optimum-effect version...

But, as Paul was wont to say from time to time, it was close enough for rock 'n' roll.

The kid actually designed a goddamned atomic bomb!

And from the looks of it, the kid also built it.

Wilson leaned over and tapped it. "That's it, Mathewson. What a nightmare!"

Mathewson shrugged and looked around the workshop with a feeling of awe, the very same feeling he had when he'd put together his own first model airplane at age seven, by himself.

"Let me talk to him first."

"But where is he?"

"I know where he is. But you'll have to promise to let me talk to him first."

"Sure. Okay," said Wilson. "Let's move." He turned to Mathewson. "So spill the beans, man."

"New York," said Mathewson. "Paul Stephens is in New York with a homemade atomic weapon."

Chapter Twenty-one

"You know, Paul," said Jenny Anderman, coming down the Deegan Expressway, "I've never driven into Manhattan before. Behind the wheel, that is."

"So?"

"It's kinda...intimidating."

"Yeah. So you want me to drive?"

"You have a license?"

"Nope."

Jenny sighed. "I guess the burden falls on me, then."

"We all must bear our crosses, Jenny."

"Yeah, but where does it say it that crosses should be atomic!"

"The Book of Bombs, chapter two, verse three: 'And the Lord spake, saying, Watch thyselves, or thou shalt blow thyselves to kingdom come!'"

"Ha ha ha!" said Jenny, avoiding the multitude of potholes in the road as best she could. "Just get me downtown, genius, and cut the preaching!"

Paul straightened the map out, but it wasn't necessary to consult it to give her instructions. He'd memorized them at a glance.

The buildings of New York reared up before them

now like a perverse science project of God's: Mutated Culture of Rock, Metal, Glass, and Paranoid Humanity.

It would win first prize any day.

The day was a beauty, sitting atop the dirt and grime of New York City like a gorgeous woman barefoot upon garbage. As Jenny's car slid through the South Bronx, across the river, into the island itself, Paul allowed himself to be overwhelmed by the immense sense of excitement that this squalid place somehow gave him.

New York was indeed a monstrous testimony to the obscenity of man's greed, pride, and insensitivity to his own humanity...but damn, it was also the City of Aspiration, the Stone Bridge to Heaven, the place where either you achieved...or you were squashed flat into the dog droppings.

How appropriate that it should be here that he should make his showing, here, the center of broadcasting, the center of Money, the Black Hole of the world.

They whooshed on down, weaving through the honking traffic, Jenny's hand's tight and stiff upon the wheel, her eyes wide as she navigated her way.

"You're doing so well," Paul encouraged.

"No, I'm not. I hate this."

Paul nodded toward all the other cars. "Most of them do it every day. Do you think they like it?"

A waft of stench waved through the open window and Jenny made a face. "What a hole!"

"You'll like the hotel."

"The Penta, huh?"

"Yeah. Classy."

"What about my car, Paul? I'm not going to leave it out on these streets!"

They were passing a stretch where natives strutted, their ghetto blasters competing with the traffic noises for attention, and doubtless Jenny felt that their eyes were fastened with fascination upon her hubcaps.

"Oh, there will be a parking garage."

"I sure hope so!" Jenny said, cutting to the right to avoid a maddened cab lurching out ahead of her.

"Here we go, Jen. Seventh Avenue."

The Penta was a huge building, tall and imposing, with a beautiful front. Paul directed her up the entrance, where the doorman stepped out to meet them.

"Guests of the hotel?" he asked, the silver buttons of his uniform shining.

"Uh-huh," said Jenny.

The doorman took out a book and wrote their license number down on a ticket, then put the stub under the windshield wiper.

"Thank you," said Jenny.

"Can't miss it. See you in a bit," said the doorman, giving them a friendly farewell salute.

They found the garage, followed the signs up the ramp, parked.

"We'll just take the bags," Paul said.

"You're going to leave"—she had trouble saying "Atom bomb," apparently—"*it?*" She looked around. "In *my* car!"

"Don't worry. It'll be fine. I just don't want to lug it around right now, till I scope out the terrain, know what I mean?"

"Okay, whatever you say."

They got out the overnight bags and Jenny's small portable typewriter and then they closed the hatchback and Paul locked it securely, slipping the car keys into his pocket.

They found the stairwell and walked down to the hotel lobby.

As soon as they stepped through onto fancy rug and beside fancy wallpaper, Paul could tell that something was going on in this hotel. The din of teenaged voices was tremendous, and the air of excitement was almost palpable.

They went through a crush of people to the registration desk, where, after a wait, Jenny was finally able to hand the check-in clerk her Visa card.

Jenny signed the receipt, and the clerk called for a bellboy to take her up to her room.

"That's okay," Jenny said. "I'll find it."

"Great," said Paul as he saw the key dangling in her hand. "I'll go ahead and register for the fair."

The lobby was jammed with all manner of kids along with the usual mix of guests, both American and foreign.

This is a long way from Ithaca, thought Paul, threading his way through the mess.

"God, Paul. Talk about a mass of eggheads!"

"Thank heavens I at least don't wear glasses," said Paul, stunned with the number of penholders in breast pockets and calculator holsters waltzing around in here.

"But you're smarter than them all combined!"

"I'm not sure I really want to be," Paul said, getting his turn at the registration table.

He pulled out his preprepared forms and handed them over to a bored-looking woman.

She examined them, consulted a list, stamped the appropriate sheets, made the appropriate entries in her log.

"There," she said blandly, collecting some stuff up in one hand. "Your exhibit will be in section thirty-nine."

She handed him his folder, stocked with goodies; then she gave him his name card.

"There's a mixer and orientation in the main lounge at one."

"Great," said Jenny. "Sounds like fun!"

"Welcome to New York," she said, her voice nasal and flat. She waved them brusquely on so that she could process the next entry.

"I think she's in a hurry so she go out and get her next dose of Demerol," said Jenny, visibly upset by the curt nastiness of the people here.

"Yeah. New Yorkers are really sweethearts inside, though. They just put up a rough front," Paul reassured her.

"Uh-huh. Sure, Paul. I'll be glad when I'm back in Ithaca."

They began to move toward the exhibition hall.

"Yeah. They all have hearts of small children. They keep them in jars on their office desks."

She laughed and punched him lightly on the arm.

The exhibition hall was on the next floor. They took an elevator, which opened up on a large auditorium, packed with booths and kids, complete with lots of curtains, a stage, and a mezzanine.

Many dozens of displays and exhibits were available on weird and different subjects, from AMAZING MICE MAZE to EFFECTS OF PHOTOGRAPHY ON MUSIC. Lots of ants, lots of computers.

Above all this was strung a large-lettered sign announcing:

NEW YORK PENTA WELCOMES 45TH ANNUAL
NATIONAL SCIENCE FAIR

Carrying their stuff, Paul and Jenny walked through.

"Hey, look who's here!" said Paul brightly.

"Oh no!"

"Let's go say hello!"

"Do we really have to?"

"Sure. Why not?"

The sign above the exhibit read: TOTAL ACCESS TO KNOWLEDGE THROUGH COMPUTERS. Bent over some machines was Roland himself, futzing about with some leads.

"Hiya, Rol!"

At the sound of that voice, Roland spun around, did a double take, and said, holding out pudgy hands, "Keep away! Just keep away from me, Stephens!"

He placed his body between himself and his beloved equipment.

Jenny smiled sweetly. "Good luck, Roland."

Roland grunted, and gave them both a very wary look as they moved on.

They were walking down an aisle, in the very center of the exhibit hall, admiring the masses of young nimble minds and their delvings into the mysterious lands of science.

"Child's play," Paul was saying.

"Oh, Paul," laughed Jenny, "get your nose out of the air!"

"Where else should my nose go, Jen?" And Paul smiled confidently at her.

Chapter Twenty-two

"Where else should my nose go?" said the guy to the pretty girl, their voices sounding tinny through the earphone.

Saito Osaka adjusted the knob, and the reception got marginally clearer. He focused his telescope, running parallel to the surveillance device—the fifteen-year-old's science project—so that he got a good picture of whom he was listening to, here above them on the mezzanine.

Gosh, the girl was really cute. He thought she'd looked cute even from a distance, and now he was real glad he'd tuned in to them. He excitedly pointed her out to his pals, other Brilliant Scientists of the Future, and then returned to his listening pleasure.

"Okay," the guy was saying to the girl. "Just before the judging, we go down to the car, sneak it up here, ask for the judge in physics, show it to him. He verifies it. We win first prize. We get lots of money, go on television, and break the story of the century, the one that will change everybody's views on the subject! Am I leaving anything out?"

The girl replied, "Just the part where we get shot for treason."

Eccles adjusted his thick-framed glasses and almost knocked off his earphones in the process. "Wow, Saito! This is great."

"Isn't it great to be a young inventor!" said Price, admiring the circular panpipe arrangement mounted on a tripod attached with a scope and a sight, seemingly more interested in it than in the sexy girl down in the hall.

Saito, though, had his priorities straight. "Would you look at her," he said, savoring this feminine visual treat. Still, they were talking about weird stuff. What the heck could this project the guy was talking about *be?* First prize? First prize, bullshit! Saito wanted first prize!

"...just think, Jenny," the guy was saying. "An atomic—"

And then they disappeared under the mezzanine.

"An atomic?" said Eccles, his eyes getting big. "An atomic what?"

"Did you hear that jerk? He thinks he's going to win first prize!"

Saito was a short, skinny genius. He didn't like being short, and he didn't like being skinny, but he liked being a genius very much and made no bones about it. Saito was from Long Island, and this was the major expedition of the year, even more important than his victory earlier this year on the *It's Academic* high school quiz show, where he had answered every question but one correctly. He had missed because he had to go to the bathroom from all the water he was drinking in the hot lights, and couldn't concentrate.

Around him were arrayed his friends from various parts of the country. They had just met the previous evening, but they had known each other for at least a year through correspondence and play-by-mail chess, a common interest among them all. Gambits and checks and checkmates had rapidly evolved into scribbled notes, then letters, about their enthusiasms. Within two months they had formed what was called an APA, a group of people collaborating on an amateur magazine consisting of stapled-together mimeoed contributions from each of the members. Saito headed this APA, and he called it the Zanies Amateur Press Association...or ZAPPA, since it was close to one of his favorite rock musicians, Frank Zappa.

As soon as they saw each other, they knew that New York City had better watch out. Last night, the Penta had barely contained their hallway shenanigans, and they'd nearly given hotel security heart attacks.

Now they were trying out Saito's project in totally degenerate and socially unredeeming manners, earphones stuck in ears, and they were all thoroughly enjoying themselves.

"Hi," said a voice beside them as they were scouting other cuties to goggle at. "What's that you got there?"

Saito almost jumped over the railing. He turned and found himself face to face with the guy they'd just been listening to...the guy talking about winning with some kind of atomic something....

"Oh, hi!" said Saito, giving them his best Japanese-American smile.

"Hi!" said the others, clearly blown away by infatuation over the arrival of this blond female vision.

"Hi," said the vision, smiling prettily.

"What's this thing?" Paul asked pleasantly.

Did they know they'd been spied upon? Saito wondered. He'd better lie. "Oh, nothing special. Just some microwaves..."

Eccles seemed particularly besotted with the girl. He adjusted his glasses and began his usual spew on what *he'd* done for *his* science project.

"I invented a way of using insects as a dietary supplement for humans. Beetles, ants, mosquitoes ...you grind them up...low cholesterol..."

Price jumped in. "Shut up, Eccles, that's disgusting." He straightened and preened. "My project, however, is quite fascinating. I took six common toads and froze them in liquid nitrogen."

"Why?" asked the blond guy.

The girl seemed curious too.

"Would you like to know!" Price said.

Dennis Moore was next. "My project is a study of social behavior in elevators ... how people act under pressure." He seemed to be scrutinizing the girl. "See?" Her eyes shifted away. He turned to her, whatever facade of self-confidence he'd worn crumbling. "Don't you like me? She doesn't like me!"

Saito shook his head wearily. "You'll have to excuse him, he's got a hormone imbalance. What's your project?"

"Oh," said the kid, his turn to be on the defensive. "Just some—uh—hamsters. Why?"

Atomic hamsters? wondered Saito.

"He's lying," said Moore. "He blinked."

"They're all afraid of the competition," said Eccles.

"Hey, what's the difference?" said the guy. "It's not if you win, it's how you play the game, right?"

"Oh, no," said Saito, "it's if you win!"

They introduced themselves.

"I'm Paul Stephens. This is Jenny Anderman," said the guy.

"Real great to meet you. Pretty far-out scene, huh?"

"Oh ... yeah. It's going to be some fair, all right," said Paul.

"So what do you think of this business of mothers trying to get rock albums labeled?" asked Saito.

"I think they should be taken out and shot!" said Paul.

"Yeah!" said the Zappas, fists raised in the air simultaneously.

"Down with censorship!" cried Eccles.

This guy is all right, thought Saito.

"Well, gotta go set up!" said Paul Stephens, putting an arm around Jenny, the lucky guy.

"Nice to meet you guys!" said Jenny, smiling sweetly, sending all the Zappas into heaven.

"Wow!" said Eccles after they were gone.

"Wow, wow!" said Saito. "Hey, chaps! I got this

feeling about those two. They're potential Zappas if ever I saw some, and they bear some watching."

"Yeah, like, this will be great for my study!" said Moore. "I can study the mating habits of teenagers."

"About as close as you'll ever get to the subject, nerd!" said Price.

"Ah, c'mon," said Saito. "We're all horny virgins, right?" His eyes narrowed. "Maybe we can get some lessons here!"

And maybe I can find out exactly what this guy is up to, he thought to himself as he returned to his surveillance of the room.

The helicopter set down upon the helipad atop the skyscraper like a bird alighting on its nest.

John Mathewson waited a moment for the blades to slow down, listening to the sound of the wind.

This could be very bad, he had decided. Or it could be over in a snap of the fingers. It all depended upon how it was handled.

He looked through the helicopter bulb to the military officers waiting for him, looking like critters out of a Godzilla movie.

"Yes, Doctor, this is very serious. We'll have to deploy all our troops and nuke the monster before he destroys Tokyo!"

"No! He's trying to say something! You must let him have his say!"

"Right. And then we blow him back to hell!"

Mathewson sighed and got out of the helicopter.

Two uniformed men braved the buffeting and met him halfway.

They headed for the elevator, down for the car that awaited them, away from the noise.

That these guys were attached to the Defense Nuclear Agency was clear by the kind of badges and medals they wore.

These guys meant business, Mathewson thought. Serious business. Hardball here.

The aide with the name Morton pinned to his chest

made the introductions. "Dr. Mathewson, Lieuten-ant Colonel Conroy from Defense Nuclear Agency."

"How are you?" said Mathewson lamely.

They got in an elevator.

"I've been better. So..." He turned and looked Mathewson squarely in the eye. "Somebody took your magic beans and built himself a firecracker, that it?"

"That's it."

"Will it work?"

"Looks pretty good on paper. Kid's got talent." And then some.

Conroy nodded. "Good. I'll recommend him for a medal if we're not all blown to hell." A cynical fellow, this Conroy, thought Mathewson. "How big a bang we talking about?"

"About fifty kilotons. Give or take."

Conroy lost his cool and went a little white. "That's not funny."

"Not supposed to be."

"Doctor, unless I'm mistaken, fifty kilotons could just about evaporate a small city."

"El Paso, maybe. St. Peterburg..."

"Good Christ. And a kid put this together?"

"Kind of makes you think, doesn't it?" returned Mathewson.

"Any idea who he's working with?"

Mathewson sighed. These military and govern-ment guys. They saw a conspiracy behind every bush. "I don't think he's working with anybody. I think he did it all by himself."

"What for?"

"I dunno. Maybe to see he could."

"That's crazy!"

"Well, it's a crazy world, isn't it?"

Oh yes, Mathewson thought as they reached the garage and headed for the Lincoln Continental. And that just about said it all!

Chapter Twenty-three

Paul Stephens sat on the hotel-room bed, tying his tennis shoe and watching Jenny Anderman spoon out the last bit of her strawberry-ice-cream soda.

On the nearby table were strewn the remnants of their room-service pig-out. They'd had coq au vin, french fries, lots of ice cream ... splurging on Jenny's Visa. Paul had promised her that all he had to do was to sell one of Richard Yates's old comics to pay her back if they didn't win lots of money here at the fair.

"You sure he'd like that?" Jenny had said.

"Ah, he'd say go for it. I mean, he did inspire me toward this, didn't he?"

"So you claim."

"Really! If not for his books and stuff ... Richard Yates is, in a very real way, right here with us!"

"So he's the one who ate the hot fudge sundae!" Jenny had said indignantly.

He looked at her. She was so interesting, in so many ways.

She was at her typewriter now, hard at work on the article she was going to sell to *Rolling Stone*.

She tossed the spoon into the glass after one last

lick, then pulled the paper from the portable type-writer.

"How's this?" she asked, and then she commenced to read:

"'Paul Stephens, a high school student from Ithaca, New York, became the first private citizen in history to join the nuclear club, an exclusive group whose other members include the United States, the Soviet Union, Great Britain, France, and China.'"

Paul looked up from his shoes.

"If I'm in the nuclear club, do I get a jacket?"

She put the paper down, got up, and sat beside him. She smiled and she smoothed his hair. After eating all that ice cream, she smelled like a Swedish dairymaid, and Paul thought it a pretty exotic aroma.

"You get anything you like."

She leaned over and kissed him, and she tasted of strawberries and cream.

He had no problem kissing back, and they caressed awhile, and Paul was reminded that it was really worth it having all these weird hormones zooming around in his bloodstream. Moments like these made it worth it.

He realized that his heart was beating like a jackhammer and that he had to do something, urgently.

"Jenny," he said.

"What?"

"I ... I never thought I'd every say this to anybody, but ..." He took a deep, excited breath. "I gotta go get the atomic bomb out of the car."

She laughed and hit him lightly on the shoulder. "Oh, you do, huh? And just leave me just like that, huh?"

"Just like that. But I'll be back."

"How about a kiss to remember me by?"

"I could be persuaded."

"Sorry. You'll have to wrestle it out of me!" Her eyes gleamed wildly with great amusement and excitement.

"Hulk Hogan meets Mr. A-Bomb!" cried Paul, and they commenced rolling about on the bed.

They did not notice, therefore, the padding of numerous feet down the hall, nor the halting of those feet outside their door, nor the insertion of a hotel passkey into their lock.

Paul vaguely caught the flash of opening door as Jenny began bouncing up and down on top of him, pummeling him mercilessly.

But he did definitely notice the five men who walked into the hotel room, several very grim-looking, very big FBI sorts, ham-sized hands very near to holsters containing guns.

One of the men was Dr. John Mathewson.

Paul, not particularly ready for this, could only manage a weak, "Hi, Dr. Mathewson!"

Jenny turned her head, said, "Yipes!" and froze.

"Paul, what the hell do you think you're doing?" demanded Mathewson, very stern, very fatherly.

"Uhmm...well, we thought we'd wrestle, then kiss some, and then move into the fancy stuff!"

"Cute," said Mathewson. "That's very cute."

Meantime, the FBI sorts had started a rather rough search of the room.

One rushed out of the bathroom. "It's not here!" he said.

One of the guys was wearing a uniform, and looking particularly silly in it, sort of a small-scale General Jack D. Ripper.

"Okay, son. Where is it?" the guy demanded.

Paul decided to try the innocent act.

"Where's what?"

"Don't try my patience, boy!" the military sort demanded imperiously.

"Excuse me," said Jenny, finally unfreezing from her startled state and getting her bearings. She stood up on the bed, looking beautiful in her wrath. "This is a *private* room!"

"Who are you?" asked the uniform.

"My name is Jennifer Anderman, and my father's a lawyer!"

The uniform said, "Good, you're gonna need him."

He pointed to the stuff near her typewriter. "Jensen! Get that."

Jenny was adamant. "You can't come in here without a warrant!"

"Yeah, what is this, Russia?" Paul demanded.

"Son," said the uniform. "Son, you have exactly ten seconds to come up with that damn thing—"

Jenny wouldn't stop. "I demand to make a phone call! They can't do this, Paul. It's illegal search and seizure!"

The uniform stepped outside to where a female FBI agent waited. Jenny strode purposefully to the telephone.

"Miss Hendrix, would you please escort this young lady outside."

"Certainly." The lady FBI agent stepped in and grabbed Jenny's arm.

"Don't you touch me!" screeched Jenny, livid.

Miss Hendrix backed off, startled by the vociferousness displayed.

"I want to know the charges!" Jenny said.

"Yeah!" Paul said, getting into the spirit, though actually feeling as though their goose were thoroughly cooked.

"Well, Conroy?" said Mathewson.

"The charges? You've got to be kidding!" The colonel seemed to loose his cool, becoming a bit red-faced. "Okay, how about theft of government property, transportation of stolen goods, reckless endangerment, violation of the Nuclear Regulatory Act, and conspiracy to commit espionage? That good enough for starters? You're in a peck of trouble, son! You're not as smart as you think...!"

Oh-oh, thought Paul Stephens. I think maybe I am.

"You're in a peck of trouble, son!" the blustery voice yelped, and Saito winced with the volume, as did the other Zappas. Price almost fell over a transceiver box, and Eccles almost lost his glasses.

"Okay, Colonel!" cried a voice. "You're not going to accomplish anything like this."

That must be that guy that looked like the scientist Saito had seen coming down the hall.

Something real weird was going on, that was for sure!

He and the crew had found out real fast that Saito's room was real close to Jenny's, and since they had plenty of eavesdropping equipment already set up...

Well, why not? Maybe they'd hear some real live making out!

Instead, they'd gotten an earful.

This little project of Paul Stephens's was atomic, all right!

It was an atomic bomb!

Far out! How had the guy accomplished this? Saito wondered, admiring him tremendously. Definitely a far greater coup even than necking with this blond beauty!

"When I want your expert advice, Doctor, I'll ask for it—" the colonel was saying.

"We demand to see a lawyer," said Jenny.

"You'll get a lawyer when I say so! Listen, I gave you an order; this isn't a goddamn debate," said the colonel.

"Get your hand away from that gun!" yelled Jenny. "What's going on here?"

Yikes! thought Saito. This is really serious.

"Okay, okay," said the scientist, yelling with enormous authority. "Everybody! Please!"

There was sudden quiet.

The Zappas' eyes were all falling out of their heads.

"Let's all get a grip, okay? Now, we did kind of burst in here....Colonel, how about me and Paul, we take a little walk, just the two of us, and try and figure this thing out? Okay? What do you say, Paul?"

"Fine."

Saito took his earplug out and motioned for the others to do so as well.

"Right, guys," he said. "I've got this great idea, and it looks like we're going to have time to do it!"

"An atomic bomb!" said Moore. "I wonder what reaction a group in an elevator would have to an A-bomb inside with them. What a fascinating sociological notion!"

"Shut up, Moore!" said Saito. "Come on, Zappas! We gotta move it!"

Chapter Twenty-four

Dr. John Mathewson sat with Paul Stephens in the hotel restaurant, his stomach churning queasily, still unable to totally believe that all this was happening.

Everything he'd worked for so long was going down the drain, and this kid, this brilliant little sixteen-year-old son of the woman he was dating, had pulled the plug!

"My gosh, can you believe these prices in this place!" Paul was saying, surveying the plastic menu.

"Yeah. Pretty steep."

The waitress came with Paul's Seven-Up and Mathewson's Coke. "That'll do, I think," said Paul.

Paul took another glance at the Feds sitting watching them over at another table.

Mathewson sighed and took a casual tack. "Kind of upset, aren't they?"

"I don't know why," said Paul sarcastically. "It's just some lubricating oil for the robot."

"What did you want us to do, put up a neon sign that said Secret Weapons Laboratory?" Hotel guests passed, and he had to lower his voice. "I wish the world were a simpler place, but it's not."

"They can't do anything to me," Paul said confidently.

"Why not?"

"I'm underage."

Sheesh, thought Mathewson, the kid really doesn't know what's going on in this country.

"That's really brilliant, Paul. What do you think this is, the school play? They don't care how old you are. Or how cute. They're gorillas. They'll hurt you, don't you get it? You try and tough it out and they'll just lock you in a room somewhere—"

Paul seemed somewhat taken back by that.

"It's really that important to you, huh?"

"Not just to me, to everybody."

Paul thought for a second, then nodded. "Okay. You can have it back."

Whew! "Okay, that's better," Mathewson said, smiling. "Where is it?"

"No, no. Not now."

Mathewson did a double take. "What do you mean, not now? When?"

"After the fair," Paul said.

"Come on, Paul!"

"But it's got to be judged. I can win first prize."

"You're putting me on!"

"No. Did you see the junk they got down there? I'm a shoo-in."

"Paul, forget the science fair. It's over, okay? No more science fair. This is top-secret stuff. Nobody gets to see it. Ever. You could start a war, for Christ's sake! Now stop screwing around—before it's too late!"

Paul frowned at that.

"I dunno."

"Look, okay, you've made your point—"

"Not the way I want to."

"Right. So ... I mean, so you got caught halfway, but it's not worth the risk, in any sense....Jeez, when I tell your mom..."

"She's never gonna see you again!" Something like satisfaction shone in the kid's eyes, and then Mathewson understood him a little better.

"Look, Paul.... This is something that happens all the time...I mean, we can deal with it over a beer or something...not a goddamned A-bomb!" He chuckled the last bit out, it was so absurd.

"There are other reasons."

"Yes, I know. Lots of reasons. You're pissed and I'm pissed and the world's a sinkhole and your pal killed himself 'cause he thought the bomb was going to drop!"

"No he didn't!" Paul said. Then he lowered his voice. "How'd you know about Richard?"

"Your Mom and I have talked about you, guy. She loves you very, very much and she told me as much as she knows. I just added a few facts together. I mean, to do this kind of stunt takes a lot of motivation!" He took a breath. "Look, you've got to understand, it's not all black and white. I mean, do you really think I'm a bad guy? Defense is an industry, Paul, and I'm just a part of that as much as the FORTRAN programmer who works out war games material on Pentagon computers! Nobody's going to really use it! It's all elaborate deterrence. Nobody wants a nuclear war! It's all shadow play!"

"You say this isn't black and white? I give you the thing, or I'm in deep trouble. Sounds black and white to me."

"Paul, Paul." Mathewson shook his head. "You're ruining your life, and any possibility of a career that will give you the kind of satisfaction I can see you need! Don't you think I haven't worked my butt off to get my hands on those lovely machines back there, show the world what I can do!"

"And get scads of money in the process."

"Living well is the best revenge."

"No," Paul said. "Dying well is."

"Paul. Paul, let's talk philosophy later! Ideals are all very well...but now we've got a pragmatic problem here! Somehow you've managed to do something no one else ever has. You've got a little item which has virtually changed the world in the past forty years into something we can barely get a handle on, and it's something which my dear friends over there would happily kill you for and then go home and eat apple pie with Mom, knowing they've once more defended the U.S. of A. Now you've got two things you can do. You can say no, in which case they'll find it anyway, people might get hurt, and you will most certainly regret this little stunt until you probably relieve your agony by following your pal to oblivion." He took a breath and met Paul stare for glare. "Or you can give it to us, and everything can get smoothed over quietly. Simple choice, eh?"

"I can start screaming right now!" Paul said.

"Paul, please," said Mathewson, playing his last card. "I'm wearing my best suit and those new explosive bullets the FBI use splatter so dreadfully."

Paul Stephens stuck the car key into the car's hatchback, twisted it, and pulled the hatch up.

He was not in the best mood, but all things considered, things could have turned out worse. Jenny would at least get her article, and he'd be interviewed and the truth about MedAtomics would get out.

Still, he wouldn't win his first prize, and worst of all, all the drama would be leached out, and he had been looking forward to that drama so very much!

The Feds hovered about him now, smelling of bay rum and gun oil, here in the New York City garage, waiting to get their sweaty mitts on his A-bomb, and he was, alas, going to have to give it to them.

He looked down into the trunk basin and immediately realized he had a little problem.

The bomb...

It was gone!

Dr. John Mathewson noticed its absence immediately.

"Paul, for God's sake!"

Two Feds grabbed him, one on either side, their grips firm and strong.

"It was here!" Paul said. "Jenny must have taken it!"

"No, the girl hasn't left the room," said one of the gorillas.

"Somebody stole it, then!" Paul said, his insides turning to mush with the very thought.

Somebody was loose in New York City with an atomic bomb!

Colonel Conroy said, "All right, son! Would you come with us now!"

"Just a minute," said Mathewson.

"That's okay, Doctor," said Conroy. "We'll take it from here."

Mathewson looked piqued. "He's telling the truth."

Paul was glad *someone* could tell.

"Fine," said Colonel Conroy. "Then he has nothing to worry about."

The gorillas started walking Paul back to the hotel.

Paul felt helpless as a baby.

"It was there! In a cat box!"

And somebody else had it!

The hotel room with the windows drawn assumed a sinister feeling, like something from a black-and-white forties spy movie.

Paul Stephens sat in the middle of that room, expecting Sydney Greenstreet to belly in at any moment. "Now, if you please, Mr. Stephens," the fat man would say, stroking the smooth head of a Maltese falcon, "where is the bomb? If you don't tell us, I shall have to set Mr. Peter Lorre here to work on you with his little item of, er, persuasion!"

And a switchblade would click out and a curly-haired psychopath would step forward into this yellow pool of light and breathe heavily as he said, "Good evening, Mr. Stephens! I hope you are ready for some fun!"

Yeah, he should be so lucky!

At least that kind of world had a Humphrey Bogart or Alan Ladd hanging around! All this one had were whacked-out colonels and horny mad scientists!

The glare from the gooseneck lamp over him was most uncomfortable.

"We really need to know where it is, Paul!" said one of the Feds.

"Shall I carve the dark or white meat first, Fat Man?" said Peter Lorre.

Paul said, "I don't know, I told you. Look, I really have to—"

He tried to get up, but two of the heavyset Feds stepped forward and slammed him back down into the chair.

"Hey! Come on! What the—"

That gleam in the light wasn't Peter Lorre's Italian switchblade. It was a very long hypodermic needle.

"Just to relax you," said a Fed.

"The gizzard first, if you please, Mr. Lorre!" said Sydney Greenstreet.

"To help you remember," continued the needle-wielding Fed.

"I told you," Paul said, "it was in the trunk!"

The needle neared, and the Fed began to look less like Peter Lorre and more like Boris Karloff.

"Okay!" said Paul, shaken. "You want the truth?"

"That's why we're here, Paul."

"The truth is you guys are a bunch of assholes and—"

Broad tape was wrapped around his mouth. He had to stop himself from choking. Had to calm down to breathe—

"You're getting a little hostile here, aren't you, Paul?"

Lon Chaney, Jr., started to roll Paul's sleeve up.

"No," said Bela Lugosi. "I can do it through his shirt."

Paul felt the sting of the needle plunging halfway into his arm, felt the pressure of it squeeze—and then it was suddenly pulled out as John Wayne and the cavalry charged into the room bearing flashlights, alarms, and fire extinguishers.

Paul struggled up, knocked over the lamp, which plunged the room into darkness.

Much confusion ensued: yelps and orders and bashing of Fed bodies into one another. The outside hall was almost in total darkness as well, and the emergency lights gave a weird glow in the nightmare-quality dimness.

Suddenly plumes of steamlike CO_2 streamed out, crisscrossed with light beams and—

And the drug pumped into Paul hit.

Things slowed down.

"Well, kid," said Humphrey Bogart, *"I brought Moe and Curly and Larry here to get you outta dis hole, so get those rubber legs under you and let's start moving!"*

"Bogie!" said Paul, the smoke and lights flashing in his face. "I built an atom bomb, Bogie, but I lost the girl!"

"Sounds like a hill o' beans ta me, kid. Now let's make this the start of a beautiful friendship."

Arms grabbed him in the confusion and pulled him out into the hallway.

"Come on!" said a kid in glasses he vaguely recognized. "We heard everything! Let's go!"

Another kid let an FBI agent have it with a fire-extinguisher blast.

The other joined them as they ran down the hall willy-nilly, the Feds far behind them.

"Is that thing really a nuclear device?" asked the guy Paul now recognized as Eccles, one of those weird guys he'd met before in the exhibition hall.

"Uh-huh," said Paul, things still moving very slowly, very confusedly.

"Far out!"

Far out, thought Paul.

"We belong dead!" said the Frankenstein Monster, *stitched-together hand reaching for the switch.*

The lights went out.

Like a spider at the center of someone's else's web—and a very wonderful, complex web it was—Saito stood in the engineering department and computer room of the Penta Hotel, engineering Paul Stephens's escape from the Feds.

Child's play! he thought, tapping away at a computer terminal.

Fortunately, he'd found this computer terminal at a science fair booth. It was labeled TOTAL KNOWLEDGE THROUGH COMPUTERS, PROPERTY OF ROLAND WORSTER, but the guy wouldn't miss it for a little while.

And it was being put to such good use!

Why, look for instance at all this delightful chaos in this huge hotel. Lights turning on and off, water spewing, elevators going nuts, fire alarms clanging, telephones ringing. Anything electronic here had just joined the rebellion bandwagon, grouping together to help their dear brother, a kid-built atomic bomb!

"The Zappas strike again!" said Saito. "They don't call us the Mothers of Invention for nothing!"

A crazed-looking fat guy caromed into the room. "That's my project!" he said. "What do you think you're doing?"

Saito held up his Venusian water pistol, which looked very much like a Magnum .44. "Care to sit down, Mr. Roland?"

Knees shaking, Roland sat down into a chair and was strapped in immediately by electrical wiring.

"There we go," said Saito, satisfied with the knot job on the rube and returning to his fun at the control board. "Simply rescuing a guy named Paul Stephens from a lot of trouble."

"Stephens!" cried Roland. "Oh no! And you've just ruined my computer and my new program!"

Saito grinned, squirted the jerk in the face, and continued jabbing away at the controls happily.

Chaos.

The science fair was something out of a Jerry Lewis film now, projects teetering, marbles rolling, electrical wires shorting....

Paul Stephens became aware of all this as he was being led along through the corridor by Eccles.

"Woody," he was saying. "You've really got to stop making these serious and meaningful movies.... Your comedies were much better...."

"What the heck are you talking about, Stephens?" asked Eccles.

"I don't know."

"Just shut up and c'mon.... Hey, there's Price with your girlfriend!"

The reunion was somewhat foggy for Paul, but Jenny did seem very pleased to see him still in one piece.

They sprinted down the steps to a service corridor in the basement where several more of the Zappa crew awaited them, wearing infrared goggles.

One of them held the cat box containing the atom bomb.

"You took it," said Paul, somewhat recovering. "How?"

"Simple. We knew the room number and tapped into the hotel computer for your girlfriend's credit-card number, and that gave us her address, and then we accessed the Department of Motor Vehicles computer for the make and license on the car!"

The room started to weave, and Paul swayed.

"We've hit an iceberg, Captain!"

"Abandon ship! Women and children first!"

Jenny's voice cut through the bleariness.

"What's wrong, Paul?"

Eccles said, "They gave him an injection—"

"Probably sodium amytal. You have a bitter taste in your mouth, Stephens?"

"Just keep him moving," said Price. "He'll be okay."

Paul was vaguely aware of being guided down the corridor amidst all the hubbub, through a fire door. Price slipped a two-by-four through the fire-door handles and they stopped a moment.

"Have you got enough money?" asked Eccles.

"For what?" asked Jenny.

"To get away," said Eccles. "The place is crawling with Feds!"

As though to punctuate this last statement, the aforesaid Feds began pounding on the barred door.

"I have a credit card," Jenny said.

"No! Come on, guys! Come on, we need some money!"

The others frantically searched their pockets, finding mostly lint and gum. Price, however, came to the rescue, pulling out a nice stack of crisp folded twenties. He peeled off four and handed them to Jenny.

"You owe me eighty dollars," he said.

One of the kids raced back, out of breath. "I got a taxi! Coast is clear!"

Paul was overwhelmed by emotion. He clasped an arm around Eccles's neck. "Bogie! Duke! You guys, you beautiful guys!"

"Okay, okay, so send me a letter!"

Jenny seemed somewhat astonished herself as she accepted the burden of Paul. "Why are you doing all this?"

Price struck a noble pose. "Because life, my dear, is more than just freezing toads."

Jenny impulsively kissed Eccles and he turned beet-red.

Meantime, the pounding from the other side of the blocked fire door increased.

"You better stop all this smooching and get the hell outta here," said Price. "I don't think Saito is going to be able to keep this up much longer."

"Yeah, and then we'll win first prize," said Moore. "For terrorism!"

"An Oscar!" said Paul. "For Best Supporting Atomic Bomb, Paul—"

"C'mon, Paul," said Jenny, and she managed to urge him into a rollicking run into the autumn New York air, ending at a cab in the street.

She pushed Paul in, then followed him onto the battered, taped seat.

The cabbie, a double-chinned, blowsy-looking guy

wearing a checkered golf hat, glanced at them with a bored expression via the rearview mirror.

"All right, folks, where to today?"

"Casablanca!" said Paul.

"Huh?"

"Ithaca!"

"Right. Funny, kid."

"Ithaca? Paul, why Ithaca?"

"Plan."

The cab moved out into deep traffic, and Paul suddenly began regaining some of his usual faculties.

They'd escaped. Wow!

"Given to you without a doubt by John Wayne and Humphrey Bogart!"

"Uh-uh. Me. I'm okay, Jenny." He leaned forward with the cat box, rapping it loudly. "Hey, mister," he said to the cabbie. "Guess what I've got in here!"

The cabbie decided to play the game. "Gee, let's see . . . a human head?"

"Wrong," announced Paul. "It's an atomic bomb. Wanna see?"

Jenny jumped in, breaking off this particular subject of discussion. "Driver, if you only had"—she counted out the spare dollars and change the others had forked over—"eighty-seven dollars and you had to get to Ithaca, what would you do?"

"Well, that's not enough for a cab!"

"No, I didn't think so."

"Well, little lady, I can get on the Hudson Parkway and whisk you on up to the George Washington Bridge bus terminal, you and your atomic bomb. How does that sound?"

"Oh, that sounds fine."

"No problem. I do great bomb carrying. Specialty."

"And we can catch a bus to Ithaca!" said Paul.

"That's the idea, Einstein," said the cabbie, cutting a sharp left and causing Paul and his case to strike the side of the cab interior.

"Hey, watch out!" said Jenny, eyes wide.

"Oh yeah. Delicate things, atomic bombs!" said the cabbie, heading down Fifty-ninth Street for the exit onto the Hudson Parkway as promised. He stuck his head out the window, and yelled. "Hey, gangway, Manhattan. A-bomb express!"

Horns honked.

"Ya see what Manhattan makes of an A-bomb. I got this theory, you see. When the Russians drop the bomb, it'll get stripped down for scrap metal before it hits ground! How's that for a good joke!"

"Uhm, fine!" said Paul, easing back into sanity, already sorry about mentioning the subject of the A-bomb he currently cradled in his lap.

"Oh, sure, I hear plenty of good jokes in this cab. How about this one: What's the drink called the Leon Klinghoffer they're drinkin' now in the Mideast?"

"Mogen David?" answered Jenny lamely.

"Uh-uh. Two shots and a splash of water. Get it?"

He laughed and almost rammed his cab into a city sanitation truck.

Many honks ensued, and Paul and Jenny began to turn an uneasy shade of green.

"What does PLO mean these days?" asked the cabbie.

Neither Paul nor Jenny had any idea.

"Pushed Leon overboard!"

They laughed because they feared they had to.

"Oh yeah, and I heard a good A-bomb joke the other day. How many Polacks does it take to make an atom bomb?"

Paul had the answer to that one. "One," he said wearily. "But he's really got to be totally crazy."

"Don't get that one," said the cabbie, and he pulled onto the Henry Hudson Parkway.

Jenny looked at Paul. "I do, Paul Stephenski."

Paul attempted a smile, but failed miserably.

Chapter Twenty-five

Earl Grey Tea.

Elizabeth Stephens loved the stuff. She poured some into the strainer and let the steamy hot water filter through the leaves, savoring the perfumy aroma that drifted up.

Paul didn't care for the stuff, even though he liked the other Twinings flavors, which Elizabeth found very odd, since he generally liked just about everything associated with Great Britain. He was an Anglophile, no question about it, and Elizabeth thought it gave him character.

She added one and a half spoons of sugar, a measure of milk, then stirred the result, letting it cool a bit before she ventured a sip, musing quietly at the countertop.

Her quiet moments... Yes, she always cherished moments such as these. Ever since her husband had galloped off, it had been quite a chore being a single mother, alimony and child support notwithstanding. Especially in those first couple of years, when Paul had been in junior high and was rambunctious and rebellious.

Thank God he had calmed down!

He was like his father in so many ways—a shame that Roger Stephens couldn't accept that, couldn't take some more time out of his life to watch his own flesh and blood grow up...

But then, Roger had always been like that. Devoted to his career first, wild times next, and a dim last, personal relationships. Even back in their early days, back at the University of Maryland School of Architecture, when she'd first had Paul before they'd been married, his evenings were spent either hunched over a drafting board, or tipping back beers at the Rendezvous Inn or the Varsity Grill down on Route One.

And hadn't those been the days? Oh yes, no makeup for her then, and Roger had affected the college uniform of the time, bell-bottom jeans, Indian shirts, and long hair. But deep down he was a proto-yuppie. Or maybe even a fifties carryover. While she had spent her time freewheeling through liberal arts, with the odd protest march or smoke-in thrown in, protesting the Vietnam War or the dorm food, he had charged like a mad bull through everything the university had to offer for his career in architecture... and when he'd swallowed everything the U of M had to offer, newly married after much pressure, he had carted wife and son to Cornell for his doctorate and the beginning of his teaching career.

The teaching had come naturally enough. Student assistantships and all that. But it wasn't long before Dr. Stephens started getting free-lance work.... And finally, the free-lance work led him into the wonderful world of Real Money, where dwelled Real Work, and Real High Living.

Elizabeth sipped at her tea.

Well, she just never should have married him. She had to take a goodly portion of the blame here. She could have just gone from the beginning being a single mother, started her own career earlier.... But in the back of her mind had always been Roger's potential. She had always believed in his other abilities, and God knows that helped him when he needed it. But her belief in his ability to change...that had never panned out.

John Mathewson...John was different.

Oh, sure, he was a workaholic, no question. He had a love for his job like nothing she had even seen. But there were things about the man that perhaps he didn't even realize he possessed, and that's what made him so charming.

Yes, she liked John. How much, God knew; she wasn't so stupid as to make any rash plunges, not after her history.

But one thing was for sure...he was a hell of a lot better than most jerks she had dated.

She put the cup back on the saucer.

A droning sound started.

What was that?

She looked out the window, into the darkness; saw a swath of light, sweeping through the trees.

Whatever is going on? she thought.

She went out to the front porch to check.

The searchlight blinded her as she looked up. It swept away for a second, and she saw the form of a helicopter descending like a Spielberg flying saucer from the starry sky. The wind from the rotor created a maelstrom, blowing the tree limbs about, scattering clouds of dust, the curtains of the open windows, her hair.

The noise was unbearable.

The helicopter hovered for a moment, and then was gone.

Then the ground vehicles showed up.

Two unmarked cars.

A van with CAYUGA POWER AND LIGHT lettered on its side.

They screeched up to the house. People got out. People wearing suits and ties...people wearing military uniforms...people looking like police SWAT team members...

And Dr. John Mathewson.

She was stunned absolutely speechless.

A man wearing an army outfit, his rank clearly

lieutenant colonel, strode up to her purposefully.
"Mrs. Elizabeth Stephens?"

"Yes?" she managed.

"Lieutenant Colonel Conroy, U.S. Army, Delta
Force. These men are from the Nuclear Emergency
Search Team, a duly authorized government agency.
Under the Atomic Energy Act I am empowered to
take over these premises as a temporary crisis cen-
ter."

The rest of the group either entered the house as
though they owned it, or started searching the pe-
rimeter with flashlights and radiation counters.

"Nuclear emergency?" said Elizabeth. "What—?"
She turned to John Mathewson.

"John, is this...? Is Paul okay?"

There was pain and a glint of fear in John's eyes.
"We think so. Something happened."

"And he was being so good!" she said.

They were called NEST team.

NEST stood for Nuclear Emergency Search Team,
a special division of the army.

They had set up shop in the Stephens living room,
and now their members, Data Nest One and Two,
Electronics Nest, Command Nest, and Utility Nest
One and Two, were systematically looking for evidence and information.

As John Mathewson walked through the elec-
tronically converted living room, a Utility Nest was
striding downstairs, carrying some magazines and
things from Paul's bedroom.

God, they were so disgustingly thorough!

A portable computer was chugging out data from
a telecommunications linkup.

Yes, just as Mathewson suspected: info on Paul.

Birth date. Place of birth. Everything.

Data Nest One was reading it off.

"Paul Jacob Stephens, born Holy Cross Hospital,
Silver Springs, Maryland, February 14, 1970. Mother,
Elizabeth Adams Stephens, twenty years old, ad-

mitted maternity ward 6:20 P.M.—given twenty-five milligrams Demerol..."

Hospital records.

"Good work," said John sarcastically. "That's gonna be real useful."

He turned away in disgust and marched to the dining room where Elizabeth was being interrogated. He hung back in the doorway for a moment and listened.

"You and your husband were separated almost five years ago, was it?" asked the man wearing a trench coat.

"Yes," said Elizabeth.

"And at any time during those years has your son had any nightmares, anxiety, or spells of depression?"

"You mean, is he normal?"

The other interrogator stepped in. "Does he eat an excessive amount of sweets?"

"Why?"

The interrogator was looking at a printout. "He got seven new cavities within the past school year and only one the prior year."

"I think we're looking at hyplogycemic mood swings with attendant paranoia," the other interrogator said.

"Does he feel that people don't like him?" asked Interrogator One.

"That's he special or different?"

"Is he unhappy with the present political system?"

Elizabeth was staring at the dental-record printout. "Seven cavities? Are you sure?"

She looked over to where Mathewson stood.

Mathewson could only shake his head and shrug. He continued on to the kitchen, where Colonel Conroy and Data Nest Two were hovering over some maps and printed matter.

Data Nest Two was saying, "These are the blast radius scenarios for all U.S. cities over half a million population, with probable strategic and psychological targets...."

On the printout of landmarks and cities were the Statue of Liberty, the Washington Monument, Mount Rushmore, the Astrodome, and other possibly threatened features of the United States.

"Now," Data Nest Two continued, in an authoritative tone, full of professional practice. "Assuming a ground burst here, our computer model estimates 90 percent structural damage within a thousand yards."

Mathewson was flabbergasted.

"Blast radius scenarios?"

"That's right."

"Paul's not going to blow anything up!"

Conroy answered that one. "We really don't know what he's going to do, do we?"

An FBI agent handed over some of Paul's stuff—papers, notebooks, magazines. He whispered in the colonel's ear. Conroy nodded.

"But he's a kid!" said Mathewson, feeling terribly frustrated.

"Yes," said Conroy. "A kid who, through your negligence, has come into possession of probably the most important scientific breakthrough of the last forty years."

"Which I discovered!" Mathewson said indignantly.

"So?"

"Well, look at it this way," said Mathewson. "The scientist giveth, and the scientist taketh away!"

"That's awfully clever," Conroy said, glaring a bootcamp DI's glare. "You think this is some kind of game?"

"I don't know exactly what it is."

"It's the survival of the civilization, Doctor. The battle for the future. Life isn't a bowl of pretty peaches and cream, Doctor, and people like you have got to get it knocked into your heads that we're involved in a conflict of tremendous scope, a game of life and death. We're talking about the only thing that can stand between the Russians and world domination!"

"Well," said Mathewson. "Now I know."

"This little prank of this little punk could cost us a twenty-year scientific lead!"

Mathewson sighed. "I hate to break this to you, Colonel, but there hasn't been a twenty-year scientific lead since Elias Howe invented the sewing machine."

Colonel Conroy flustered at that one.

"And has it occurred to you, Doctor, that your little protégé is out there running around like some kind of...manual of mass destruction, just waiting to be picked up and read by anyone at all? And I'm not talking about the Russians or the Chinese; here they don't worry me. It's the little guys give me the whimwhams...the towel heads...the wogs...any self-styled lunatic who wants to hold the world hostage. ...It could all come apart. Don't you realize that?"

Mathewson said, "Well...I'm just a scientist. I leave the politics to experts like yourself."

"Just a scientist?" said Conroy. "Listen here, pal. Nobody's *just* anything. We're all in this together, and we've all got to choose our sides or get stamped out in the shuffle. Now, are you in here with us or not? Do you want to get this little toy out of your little friend's playful mitts?....Or do you want to take a little trip and tell my superiors why you don't? Hmmm?"

"Look. Of course I want to get the thing...and my stuff...back. I'm just saying that no way is Paul the kind of villain you think him to be!"

"I don't have the leisure to think that way, to take that chance, Doctor. All contingencies must be allowed for!"

Mathewson's eyes rolled heavenward.

So nice to meet the people you worked for, so very nice.

Chapter Twenty-six

The Trailways bus rolled along through the New York State night, powering sleekly over the highway toward Ithaca, situated by the Finger Lakes in the central region.

Paul Stephens slept.

It had been a long day, and as soon as they had gotten out of the New York City region, realizing they had indeed escaped for the time being from the authorities, both he and Jenny had calmed down, and dropped off to drowses.

But in his sleep, Paul Stephens dreamed, and he dreamed of a mushroom cloud and a roar like a planet cracking apart, and the light of a thousand suns melting eyes to slag.

Paul woke.

He started, not realizing where the hell he was at first. Then the sight of Jenny, in the window seat, sound asleep, and the sound of the wheels rumbling over macadam brought it all back instantly.

The cat box.

He checked for it, and yes, it was still under the seat.

Whew!

He rubbed his eyes, refocusing on everything. The bleariness was gone, and damn, his arm hurt from that rough injection. But he was sharpening up quick, which meant the effects were wearing off. He was going to be okay.

The bus was only half-full, and most of the people sat up front, which was why he and Jenny had chosen the back, where the toilet sloshed, smelling of disinfectant.

A flickering of light attracted Paul's attention.

Two seats up, on the other side of the aisle, a fat man slumped, asleep. Resting on his protuberant stomach was a portable battery-powered television set. No one sat next to the guy either. An earphone cord dangled down the side of his head, as though his brains were leaking out.

Paul was going to turn away and check with Jenny on something, when something flashed across the screen of that TV that galvanized him.

It was a picture, and he knew that face.

It was *his* face!

It was him, in a school picture. Soccer team, wearing shorts and shirt. Below it was the legend TEEN-AGE TERRORIST.

Cripes!

He went across the aisle, double-checked to make sure no one else was watching the TV newscast. Then carefully he plucked the earphone from the ear of the fat guy and stuck it in his own ear.

"...the boy," the announcer was saying, "whose name is being withheld, is sixteen years old and from Ithaca, New York. Federal authorities in several states are looking for him and a companion, who are wanted for questioning in what appears to be a rather unusual burglary case."

Paul felt a tap on his shoulder, which almost caused him to hit the roof. He turned and saw that it was only Jenny with a what's-going-on? look on her face.

He stabbed a finger at the TV set, and held the earpiece so that even though it cut the volume down to a little tinny voice, they both could hear the newscaster.

Who said:

"Although official sources refuse to comment, indications are that before it's over, this story may deeply compromise the American defense community, with overtones of espionage and perhaps even violations of international treaties. Barbara Collins has more in New York, where this all began at the National Science Fair."

The lady reporter identified herself. "I'm here at the Penta Hotel, the scene of a great disturbance at the National Science Fair. As you can see, all is chaos here, after the escape of one Paul Stephens who allegedly brought a nuclear device to enter in the fair and eluded apprehension by the authorities. I'm talking right now to one of the students attending the affair, Roland Worster. Roland, I understand you know Paul Stephens. What is your assessment of him?"

And yes, there he was, the fat SOB, right on TV.

"Stephens? Very disturbed person. Definitely the disturbed type."

Jenny gasped. "That— You know where I'd like to stick your cat box, Paul?"

Paul was afraid to ask.

"Uh, mister?"

The bus driver looked up into the rearview mirror, saw Jenny and Paul and the cat box.

"Yeah."

"You could do us a big favor. I live in the farmhouse just a little bit down the road, and there's no one at home to come and pick us up. I was wondering if you could just drop us off here."

The bus driver thought about it a moment. "Against the rules, miss."

"Oh dear, Paul, do you think Satan can wait?"

"I don't know. The hinges are straining, Jenny," Paul said, looking down at the box in his hand as though filled with fear.

"Satan?"

"Yes, Satan's my twenty-one-foot-long python, and we had to stick him in this cat box, and he barely fits, and I don't think he likes it very much!"

The bus pulled off onto the shoulder of the road. The driver levered the door open.

"Bye," said the driver.

"Gee, thanks!" they said, stepping out into the night.

The bus pulled away.

"Okay," said Paul. "Down the road...I know this neat place where we can gather our wits."

"What few are left," said Jenny.

Suddenly, from the distance came the sound of sirens.

"Oh-oh," said Jenny.

Across the field came flashing lights.

"Oh-oh," said Paul. He grabbed her arm and led her up a small road stretched out across a field.

They raced up a hill. The top offered a view of farm buildings.

"That barn. That's it," said Paul.

Once they reached it as quietly as they could, Paul picked the lock. They entered the straw-musty semi-darkness.

"What are those?" asked Jenny.

"Gro-lites," said Paul. "Up here. In the loft."

"Uh-uh. Mom warned me about country boys like you."

They climbed up to the loft and settled into a place that offered some concealment.

They were quiet for a while, regaining their breath. Paul didn't think about much of anything; he was too wrapped up in his plan.

Then Jenny said, "Uh, Paul, listen—"

"What?"

"Let's just give it back."

"Tomorrow," Paul said.

"What are you gonna do?"

"Get you your article."

"I dunno, it's getting too big."

"Don't give up now. Not when we've got 'em."

"We've got *them?"*

"Sure. Come on—if it was easy it'd be easy.... What about nobody doing anything, remember? And the future; what about all that?"

"If we get killed we won't have any future."

"Of course we will. You always have a future. And if worse comes to worst, we'll have posterity!"

"Kiss my posterity!" she said. "I'd like to live a little longer!"

Suddenly the sound of a helicopter whooshed over the roof of the barn. Lights from passing cars shone through the slats of the barn, exposing the plants, creating odd and crazy patterns on the walls.

Paul put a protecting arm around Jenny. She relaxed against him, trusting, and he knew she'd be okay, she'd stick with him through this whole thing.

A distant siren sounded.

"Hey," said Paul. "Want an apple?"

She shook her head. Paul got one out of his sack and bit into it.

He was going to need his strength tomorrow.

No question about that.

Chapter Twenty-seven

Dawn touched the Stephens household lightly, just waking up.

The people in the house—the Feds, Lieutenant Colonel Conroy, Elizabeth Stephens, and Dr. John Mathewson—had never gone to sleep.

Mathewson sat now holding a small glass prism of Paul's above the mess from the Feds' search. Elizabeth was attempting to straighten it all up, a look of weariness and worry tightening and lining her face.

"I'm just saying," Mathewson told Elizabeth, "that it might be easier if you accepted that he wasn't an innocent victim in all this."

"Yes, I know, he's the criminal. That makes it all so simple," said Elizabeth.

The sound of walkie-talkies crackled from the porch.

"He did do some things that are against the law. You've got to admit that," said John, imploring her to understand.

Elizabeth wasn't buying it. "Maybe there's a higher law."

"A what?"

"A higher law."

As gently as he could, John said, "What, are you saying he did it for ethics? For reasons of conscience? Who do you think he is, Galileo? He's a kid. I don't buy this Richard Yates bull at all. Kids don't have reasons. They just do things."

Elizabeth glared at him. "What do you know about children?"

"I used to be one."

"You don't know him!" Elizabeth shot back.

"Oh, but I do. He's got a gift, and he wants to use it, that's all. It's a natural thing, like breathing. Don't turn him into some kind of activist."

Elizabeth was trying to light a cigarette and she couldn't get one to light, her hands were shaking so badly.

She flung it all down and started to come apart.

"What... what's wrong?" John said, going to her but not knowing what to do.

"Who are these people? They're in my house! What gives them the right? They know about everything ... they even know about his teeth!"

He put a hand on her arm, and she jerked away, trembling. She sat down, gathered up her cigarette, matches, and managed to get it lit. She took a long drag, let out a plume of smoke.

"Why don't you *do* something, for God's sake?"

"What do you suggest?" John said.

"I don't know. Blow the bastards up. That's your field, isn't it?"

John did not respond immediately.

When he did so, he spoke evenly and as rationally as possible.

"He's a very resourceful boy, I'm sure he'll be okay."

"I hope so, because... if anything happens to him—" She turned on him, and her eyes were red and swollen. "Anything! If one hair on his head... is harmed... I promise you, I'm going to find all of you people... and... and I'm going to make your lives absolutely miserable."

Mathewson looked away.

He didn't know how he could tell her that his life already was miserable.

The phone rang.

Elizabeth picked it up.

"Hello?... Who?... Yes, I'll accept.... Hello, Paul?"

Lieutenant Colonel Conroy, previously dozing in an overstuffed chair, stepped over to a phone-tap machine, picked up earphones, and began to listen.

"Hi, Mom. Don't get crazy."

"Paul, what's going on? They're saying all kinds of things—"

The other Feds were listening by now. Mathewson, walking downstairs after a trip to the toilet, quietly picked up one of the earphones.

"Look," said Paul over the phone. "I'm okay, but I don't have much time; I have to get a message to John. So if he calls—"

"I'm here, Paul," said Mathewson.

"What?"

"It's me, Paul. John."

"You're there in the house?"

"They're all here, Paul," said his mother.

"Who all?"

"Lots of government men, the army... it's like an invasion...."

"Jesus. Are you okay?"

"Yes. Are you going to give them what they want?" she said slowly.

"Yes, I am," said Paul.

Relieved looks were exchanged around the room.

"But I want something in return," continued Paul.

"What?"

"A statement."

"What kind of statement?" asked John.

"From you, John Mathewson. Signed by you, about the lab. What it is, where it is, what happens inside, everything."

"But what for?" asked John.

"I just want it."

"I can't do that," said Mathewson. "I've signed a security clearance. I'll go to jail, you'll go to jail—"

"Look, that's the deal. The gadget for the statement. Come on, I don't have a lot of time."

Mathewson looked around helplessly.

Conroy nodded to him.

"Okay, Paul," said Mathewson. "What do I do, type something up?"

"That'll do for starters."

"Starters?"

"Just meet me in one hour at the lab. Main gate."

"The lab. Why the lab?"

"Because that's what I want. And make sure we can get inside. I want photographs, too."

"Photographs? Come on, Paul—"

"Yes! That's right, lots of photographs! And I tell you, pal, no funny stuff. I'm very tense and there's no telling what I might do."

"Paul!" said his mother. "This is crazy."

"You're fine!" said Mathewson. "Take it easy."

"No! I'm a terrorist. Haven't you been watching television?"

"What? What are you talking— Paul?" said Mathewson.

There was a click.

He was gone.

Mathewson ran down the stairs, putting on his jacket, holding the letter he'd just typed in his teeth.

Lieutenant Colonel Conroy intercepted him.

"We can arrange for someone else to give that to him, Mathewson."

Elizabeth handed him an envelope. He stuck the folded letter inside, sealed it carefully, then looked up at Conroy.

"No. He trusts me. Let me do it. I'll get it back. That's what we want, isn't it?"

"And how do we know this thing won't be armed?" Colonel Conroy asked pointedly.

"Armed?"

"That's right. He used the phrase 'I'm a terrorist.'"

He consulted a piece of paper, reading. "... 'No! I'm a terrorist. Haven't you been watching television?'"

"You people really live in your own paranoid world, don't you?"

Conroy stiffened. "We don't have the luxury of living in yours."

Elizabeth was silent as Mathewson went to her.

"I promise you, Elizabeth, I'll bring him back. Everything will be just fine."

She was staring out the window. "That'll be a change, then."

He touched her. "Really. Don't worry. I...I care for you, Elizabeth."

She said nothing.

"Well, I trust that one of these many vehicles of yours is capable of giving me a lift, Colonel?" said Mathewson.

"I think that can be arranged," said Conroy.

Chapter Twenty-eight

The ancient black pickup truck rattled down the road, Paul Stephens and Jenny Anderman bouncing in the cab seat.

They'd woken up before dawn, eaten apples, and then Paul had found this rattletrap nearby. Using Jenny's ever-handy nail clipper ("It's getting somewhat like Doctor Who's sonic screwdriver, isn't it?" Jenny had offered) to help him hot-wire the thing.

They'd halted long enough at a truck stop to call his house and make their demands.

Now they were headed for their rendezvous with John Mathewson.

Paul pulled off the road, stopped, and accepted Jenny's camera.

"Okay," he said. "It'll take me about five minutes to walk to the gate. You know what to do?"

Jenny nodded. "Drive to the bait shop and make the call."

"You got change?"

"Yes. Don't worry. I'll do it."

She was looking at him strangely.

"What else?" he asked.

"Don't...don't forget to focus."

"Piece of cake."

She looked like she wanted to say more...a great deal more.

Paul could feel something deep tugging in him as well as he looked at her, looked at the way she looked at him...those eyes, those beautiful eyes...

She leaned over and kissed him, slipping her arms around him and holding him tightly.

He didn't want to let go.

But he did. He let go and he picked up the cat box holding his own personal atomic bomb, and he waved good-bye to Jenny Anderman.

Maybe for a very long time indeed, he thought.

Dr. John Mathewson waited by the gate area of the MedAtomics building, holding a walkie-talkie.

The place was surrounded by state troopers at checkpoints. The doctored rifles of SWAT team sharpshooters stuck out like pins from bush and tree cushions.

The first roadblock was a quarter mile up the road, out of sight, and Mathewson was waiting for a message from them.

It crackled over the walkie-talkie.

"This is Unit One. The package has arrived."

Which meant that Paul was now walking up to them, past them, toward Dr. John Mathewson.

Mathewson patted his jacket pocket. Yes. The letter had not fallen out.

Another message crackled over the transceiver: "Copy, One. Okay. All units. Pass him through."

Mathewson took a deep breath and he thought about all this, and what it meant. Then he opened his channel of the walkie-talkie. "I'll be right back. Call of nature."

He walked across the road, and he thought of the years he had spent struggling for some kind of recognition in the scientific community. He thought of the things he had given up; he thought of the late hours he might have been with friends or with dates, or with a wife and family, that he had given to this and other related projects, yearning, yearning for the gold ring.

And now this kid ... this astonishing sixteen-year-old, this Paul Stephens ... had dashed that gold ring from his hand.

John Mathewson went behind a tree, out of view, and he threw up what he had been able to eat for breakfast.

When he was finished, he hurried back to his checkpoint and he waited for Paul Stephens, breathing through his nose, calming down, calming down.

When he walked down the road, Paul was wearing the same clothes he was wearing yesterday, although much scruffier now, of course. The rifles bristled from their hiding places as Paul Stephens walked down the road with almost a serene gait.

It was on his face too. A purpose. A goal.

What was going on with this guy?

As he approached, though, Mathewson could see the terror in Paul Stephens's eyes, and that made him all the more human, all the more frightening.

"Hi," said Mathewson.

"Hi," said Paul.

It was one of those beautiful fall days when the sun struggles out one more measure of gold, somehow more beautiful with the new, fall colors in the trees. There was a weird stillness to the air, an eerie silence punctuated from time to time by the rattle of weapons.

"That it?" asked Mathewson, nodding down at the thing in Paul's hand.

"Uh-huh."

"What's that, a cat box?"

Paul nodded.

"Have you got the statement?" Paul asked.

Mathewson slipped it out from his pocket, showed him.

"Could you open it and hand it to me, please?"

Mathewson opened it, gave the letter to him, and Paul took a moment to read it.

"Very good. Okay, let's go."

Paul was looking past the gate, toward the MedAtomics building.

John was shocked. "You don't really want to go inside the building."

"Oh yes."

"Paul...it's dangerous!"

"I gotta have photographs."

Mathewson shrugged, and suppressed a shudder.

He glanced up at the Command Nest, where the sun was glinting off the parabolic reflector of a long-range listening device.

Oh yes, they were hearing everything.

"Okay."

They walked toward the gates, and the gates opened for them.

As they walked down the approach road Mathewson said, "Paul, why the big push for publicity?"

"Well," said Paul, "I was thinking. This is such a neat place that people ought to know about it."

"What?"

"No, really. Lots of cool equipment...robots... *plutonium!* ...Why keep it a secret? They should have tours, like Disneyland."

"Paul, you may be having...fun...at the moment, but I promise you, these people—"

Paul shot a glare at him. "I'm not having fun!" He looked away and he took a deep breath and he let it out raggedly. "I'm scared out of my mind." Another swallow of breath. "But I don't really have a choice."

"Of course you do. Give me the box."

"And then?"

"And then...we all go home."

"You think they're just gonna let me go home knowing what I know about this place? Jesus, you're more naive than I thought," Paul said, looking more skittish by the moment.

"So what do you think they're going to do?"

Paul laughed and pointed wildly about at all the men, all the guns. "I think they're going to try to kill me."

Mathewson's voice got small. "Why on earth would you think that?"

"Because that's what I would do in their place. If I had their jobs."

"Come on, that's purely hypothetical."

"Why? I'm the leak. Plug the leak. Perfectly logical."

"Well, then—what are you going to do?"

Paul checked his watch. "Gonna spread the news."

He looked up, and there were Feds and military sorts and all manner of official-looking folk suddenly crawling out of the woodwork.

A helicopter landed nearby and more SWAT team personnel disembarked.

Together they walked into the reception and security area of MedAtomics.

"Oh, good!" said Paul. "A party!" He glanced at all the guns, all the khaki, all the boots, the grim expressions. "Doesn't look like the Communist party, though, does it? Hi, guys, did Ronnie come, or is he taking a nap?" He smiled. "I know why you're so freaked about this place." He grinned over at Lieutenant Colonel Conroy. "This is where you're keeping Adolf Hitler in suspended animation!"

"Paul!" said Mathewson.

"Well, Dr. Mengele. Vee go, *ja?*"

Oh, God, thought Mathewson. He really does want to get himself shot.

She just hoped this plan worked, because if it didn't...

Jenny Anderman trembled slightly at the very thought, and shoved it promptly from her mind as she sighted the outdoor phone booth by the bait shop.

The location offered a beautiful view of the lake, but Jenny hardly noticed the mirror blue ridged with green, the fall-touched hills, as she pulled the truck off the road and got out.

She had to call Max.

Max Perkins. Both she and Paul knew they could trust Max Perkins. Max was the school activist. Her dad had helped him out of jail once, when he'd staged a sit-in protesting the school's policy on minorities. In the age of hardhearted yuppies hot for their MBAs and their condos, Max was really quite a guy, a guy who worked for the causes he believed in. For instance, he'd been working on the Ethiopian famine relief long before Michael Jackson had ever heard about it and jumped on the bandwagon.

Yes, thought Jenny. They could count on Max Perkins.

She got out her phone-number book, slipped a quarter in the phone, and dialed the number.

She'd known Max for years. His parents were tight with hers . . . like Jenny, he'd gotten his activist leanings from them, because they too had worked for causes in the sixties.

Nope, the Perkinses hadn't sold out, she thought as the phone rang.

A guy answered.

"Hello?"

"Max! Thank God!"

"Jenny?" There was excitement and worry in his voice.

"Yes!"

"Jesus, what's going on? You guys've been on the news, and somebody said there was a helicopter at Paul's house."

"Listen, Max. You gotta do two things for us, okay? It's a matter of life and death—"

"Sure. Whose?"

"Everybody's! First, call my parents, and then—you listening?"

"Yeah! Yeah! Go ahead!"

"Call two people, and tell them to call two people! We'll contact the whole town!"

"But what will I tell them? What should they do?"

And Jenny told him their plan.

Chapter Twenty-nine

The government people watched Paul Stephens cart his nuclear weapon toward the lab, accompanied by Dr. John Mathewson.

Abe Turkel, designated Nest One, spoke into his walkie-talkie tersely. "This is Position Two. They're coming through. Approaching the detector." The adrenaline had long since kicked in on Turkel's system, but he didn't like it much this time. This was serious shit. A kid with an atom bomb. Sheesh!

At the Command Nest in the lobby of MedAtomic, Luke Meeker took the call. "Okay, Position Two. We copy." He stuck another piece of gum in his mouth and leaned over to the CRT monitor, waiting. The next minute would tell the tale.

Lieutenant Colonel Conroy and his aide, Morton, chose that opportune moment to arrive, and they checked that screen as well.

Another screen showed Mathewson at the checkpoint. He produced his key-card, slid it through. The door opened, and the two of them entered together into the main lab corridor.

"He's about to hit the pass-through detector, sir," said Meeker.

"Good. You've got it set up?" asked Conroy.

"You bet."

"He won't be alarmed, will he?"

"He's not stupid. He knows there's a radiation detector there. That sound will mask what's really going on."

"Yes, sir."

Luke's hands played with the controls, putting up the necessary views on the screen. One screen showed a close-up of a black cylindrical protuberance about the size of a soup can. The kid was approaching it.

That would do it, thought Meeker. That would do the trick!

On the main screen, the tracking camera showed a close-up of the cat box, with Paul's hand clutching the handle tightly. As he passed through the detector, a light sprang on—

A high-pitched beeping could be heard in the distance.

Another camera showed Paul, alarmed.... He looked around and seemed to indeed realize he had triggered the radiation detector.

He continued.

What he did not realize was that he had also triggered an X-ray camera, and the X-ray photo was now frozen in the main monitor.

Showing:

A fluoroscope image of the shot of the cat box and handle and hand. The hand was skeletal: like the hand of death. Inside the ghostly outline of the box, in clear negative images, were the contents of the gadget. The core, the trigger device, the plutonium. All of it.

Meeker looked it over.

"He's got it, all right. There's the core; there's the explosive package, electronics... tamper. Nice design."

Colonel Conroy went to the heart of the matter.

"Is it armed?"

"Nope." And what a relief too, thought Meeker.

"You certain?"

"Uh-huh. All in sections."

"Wonderful! We've got him!" said Conroy.

Paul Stephens was almost there. He had to buy more time...time seemed such a precious thing now. If he could stall...

But time slipped by with incredible slowness. Glacial...

There it was, Master Atom's Kitchen. The huge MedAtomics lab, better lit this time than the last time Paul Stephens was here.

Bubble, bubble, toil and trouble, he thought perversely.

The cat box and its contents seemed terribly heavy now, leaden.

He just prayed that Jenny had made that call, and that right now calls were going all over Ithaca.

They were in the hallway now, almost to the next door.

And a voice, like the voice of some metallic god, sounded from behind them.

"Paul," it said. "Would you turn around, please?"

Paul turned around, as did Mathewson.

Just a few steps away was a SWAT team member. He wore a big bushy mustache, khakis, and a headset. In his hand was an automatic weapon of some sort.

He said, "We know it's not armed, so just put it down and walk away, okay?"

Damn! thought Paul, feeling the adrenaline flowing through him. They must have somehow X-rayed the box! They knew!

He considered what he could do next, short of getting himself wasted.

Apparently Mr. Swat was quite an impatient man who did not like to wait.

"I'm gonna count to three. One...two..."

Paul said, "Aw, shit."

And he bolted past Mathewson for the lab doors.

"Paul!" cried Mathewson, reaching for him but missing. *"No!"*

The sprint put Mathewson directly between the SWAT team gorilla and the fleeing Paul, and Mr. Swat clearly did not care for the situation much.

He lunged forward, hauled the scientist aside, took aim with his gun.

"Stop," he said, "or I'll shoot."

Paul held the box close to his chest as he ran. It was his ticket out of here. They couldn't hit the box.

Another SWAT guy appeared at the far end of the corridor.

"No," cried Mathewson. "You lunatics! It's plutonium!"

You tell the bastards! thought Paul, holding the box so that there was no clear shot at him without hitting it.

"Don't hit the box!" cried a voice over the intercom system.

"Jesus!" said Colonel Conroy's voice in the background. "Hold everything. I'm heading for the lab!"

Paul ducked into the nearest corner, still holding the box at chest level. The first SWAT team member had his gun up and was aiming!

"Bastard!" cried John Mathewson, lunging on the guy, hauling his arm down.

Ka-bamm!

The sound of the wild shot was deafening in the corridor as it ricocheted off a metal wall.

Mathewson kicked the SWAT guy hard and then stepped over to the side of the hall. With a swipe of his hand, he hit a switch that plunged the corridor into shadow.

Paul didn't need to be told what to do. Holding tightly on to the box, he ran a zigzag pattern down the hall, plunging through the doors of the main lab.

Here he would have some cover!

Sergeant Ron Dalrymple was livid with anger.

He recovered his balance. He stepped forward and he rammed his hand up the wall, turning the goddamned lights on. With some illumination on the subject, he grabbed hold of the asshole doctor who'd just messed things up. He banged Mathewson against the wall and stuck the muzzle of his rifle against the jerk's temple.

"Hands on the wall, Doctor," Dalrymple growled. "You breathe funny, I'll blow your fucking brains out!"

Meanwhile, Paul ran through the lab toward the plutonium storage area.

He ducked behind one of the big machines, wedging himself into a corner.

A SWAT team member tried to draw a bead and failed. "There's no way I can get him without hitting that green stuff," he said into his headset transmitter.

"Me neither," said another one, who had just burst through the main lab doors and scuttled behind a machine.

"Same here," said another.

Lieutenant Colonel Conroy rushed into the hallway, where Sergeant Dalrymple had Dr. Mathewson pressed against the wall. He peered through the hall window with a pair of binoculars.

"Oh boy," he said.

"What?" asked Mathewson.

Conroy took a sharp breath. "Now he's really putting it together."

Chapter Thirty

He was putting it together.

Detonator assembly, implosion trigger, aluminum bulb of plutonium: it all fit like clockwork, just as before, when he'd tested it out in the Ithaca High School workshop under the cover of working with hamsters.

He never thought it would come to this.

He screwed the plug in and put the timer on, set it.

There. It was armed. The bomb was armed.

Come and get me, you bastards, he thought scrunched up against the cold metal. Come and get me, you cold machines, 'cause I've got a better machine than you, and if this machine goes, this whole place goes, all this plutonium and all, and you'll go with it!

He huddled there in the corner, his atomic bomb armed, and he held his hands up and they were shaking.

Paul Stephens took a deep breath and put his hand back down on the bomb, clenching his teeth, biting his lip until it bled.

They couldn't see he was scared. He couldn't tip

them off, the regimented Reagan clones. You come and get me, Duke, get your cancer-ridden lungs blown to hell. That's right, Rambo, I've got you by your red-white-and-blue balls! Yo, Rocky! Pal, you're down for the fucking count!

He took a few deep breaths, trying to calm down. From here, he could see the snouts of the automatic weapons pointing from various places, and he knew he was okay for the time being, because if he wasn't, these robots would have gotten him by now.

Oh, their eyes...their eyes were brainwashed! Brainwashed! This country, this culture! Brain-washed! The American Way! Program thy children to be good ass-kicking, blue-eyed, money-earning Nazis!

Why not just do the human race a favor! he thought, looking about at this Dr. Frankenstein's laboratory of death, this worm in the heart of his beautiful Ithaca. Yeah. He wasn't getting out of here without a few dozen slugs in his brain anyway. He was a goner, that was for sure.... He knew that now.

His whole idea of getting others to help...what a joke! It was all a joke, a joke that had blown up in his face...

And a tiny nudge of his finger could make it blow in theirs!

Whoops! There goes Ithaca High! Bye-bye, Wilke! Farewell, Roland! And with a good draft east, this little blast would get Wall Street and the yuppies!

A southern push of the old north wind would get Washington, D.C.

Oh, dear, what a terrible accident, the world would say. Ronald Reagan, D.C., and New York City, gone!

Boo-hoo!

Paul Stephens chuckled and a tear came to his eye, but it wasn't a sad tear.... At the core of tragedy was a joke.... That was what Richard said. "You just have to read your Jean-Paul Sartre."

He thought of Richard, and his British folk mu-sic—the words and music of hundreds of years of birth and death, war and love—and he remembered a song off the most recent Battlefield Band album, called "The Yew Tree."

This yew tree, it seemed, had seen a lot of shit, a lot of bad stuff, on the grim border between Scotland and England, and the singer knew that it was suffering from all the blood it had sucked through its rugged roots, and perhaps should be felled:

*But a wee bird flew out from your branches
And sang out as never before,
And the words of the song were a thousand years long
And to learn them's a long thousand more.*

Oh, my God, he realized. What have I done?

And Paul Stephens thought, I'm as bad as they are.

He laughed again, and he knew that no way was his finger ever going to get *near* that trigger. His blood could well be splattered all over this place... and maybe he deserved it.

And maybe, also... maybe all this stuff could just work.

He was still sucking in air. As long as he was here, and they were there, and they were scared shitless, then there was a chance.... And that chance depended on Jenny and the people of Ithaca....

Jenny. Yeah, Jenny. He'd forgotten about her in his terror and his anger, and even at the very thought of her, he knew very well he could never have set off this bomb.

It certainly wouldn't do much for her creamy complexion!

And besides, his mom would kick his butt in the hereafter.

He grinned to himself, and held his bomb very close, though suddenly it seemed very alien to him, as though someone else had made it, not him.

No, he thought, holding its coldness close. Not him.

* * *

"Mrs. Stephens?"

"Yes?" Elizabeth could not hide the strain in her voice.

"It's me. Jenny."

"Jenny! Paul! Where's Paul?"

"He's fine. But he needs your help. He needs all our help. I've been calling people, and I figured to leave you for last, 'cause you've got all those military types hanging on you."

"They're gone now, Jenny. I'm here alone."

"Fine. You have a car?"

"Oh, sure."

"Good. Well, I want you to head down to Med-Atomics. I've ordered up a town meeting down there, and I don't want you to miss it."

"I'll see you there. . . . And, Jenny?"

"Yeah?"

"Thanks, Jenny."

"Sure."

She hung up, got her car keys, and headed out for the station wagon.

Sure enough, coming down main street were cars . . . and kids! Kids on bikes! Zooming down the hill toward the lake and MedAtomics!

She felt a thrill of community to see such a sight. She turned the ignition, put the car into gear, waited her turn in traffic, and joyfully joined them.

They were in a monitor area, overlooking the main lab from a high angle.

Lieutenant Colonel Conroy. Lieutenant Morton. Supervisor Wilson.

Dr. John Mathewson.

Mathewson could see Paul down there, curled into a ball, holding the bomb like the shield it was to him. That bomb, holding his plutonium, amongst all his plutonium in their racks, his special Brand XXX plutonium . . .

"All right," said Lieutenant Colonel Conroy. "Here's the deal. We've got an irrational child down there with an armed device. He seems to trust you, Doctor. So you get down there."

"And do what?" Mathewson wanted to know.

"Disarm it. Get him to take it apart."

"And if he won't?"

"Then separate him from it and we'll do the rest."

The colonel said that with grim, clipped tones.

God, thought Mathewson. And I'll bet they'll take a lot of pleasure in doing the rest!

"I can't do that!" he said.

"Why not?"

"I'm not a...a..."

Mathewson groped for the right word.

"Killer?" said Conroy, supplying it. "Is that the word you're groping for, Doctor? And what the fucking hell do you think you've been working on all these years? What do you think all this is *for?* A square dance?"

He gestured out at the lab.

"You're a son of a bitch, Doctor," said Conroy. "Just like the rest of us. Now for God's sake take some responsibility and do what has to be done!"

"Very well," said Mathewson. "Whatever you say, Colonel."

He went down to the main lab, and the lieutenant colonel cleared his way via communications.

Mathewson walked through the main lab doors and then around so that he could see Paul. He held out his hands, attracting Paul's attention, showing him he meant no harm.

He walked slowly to him, and sank down against a wall a few feet from the kid and his atomic bomb.

"Hello again," he said.

"Hi," said Paul, easing his grip on the oblong thing just a bit, revealing the timer to John.

"Two minutes. Playing it kind of close, huh?"

Paul shrugged.

Mathewson pointed. "What's that, a Volkswagen key?"

"Uh-huh," Paul responded diffidently.

"Very interesting." And it was ... in a strange way. "And the reflector?"

A smile tugged at the corner of Paul's mouth. "Salad bowls."

"Salad bowls! And why not?"

He rubbed his unshaven jowl thoughtfully, then added:

"So what do you say we take it apart before everybody goes crazy?"

"I'm sorry, I can't do that right now."

"This isn't accomplishing anything."

"Sure it is," said Paul promptly.

"What?"

"Deterrence."

"What?"

"Deterrence," Paul repeated. "You know, like when each side thinks the other guy's gonna blow everybody up? It's actually called Mutually Assured Destruction."

"I know what it's called," said Mathewson.

"Well—it's working. I mean, I'm still alive, right?"

"Don't talk like that," said Mathewson.

"The only thing is," said Paul, "I've been thinking about it ... and I'm not sure I'm crazy enough to really turn the key."

Paul shuddered, looking right on the edge of something ... but keeping tight control.

Something pressed inside Dr. John Mathewson, pressed something deep, so deep he didn't know he'd had something like this inside him before ... right beside his feelings for Elizabeth.

"That's the flaw, isn't it?" he said.

"So," said Paul, looking down at the atomic bomb in his lap as though it were some cancer growth blooming from his stomach. "When you come right down to it, I guess I blew it." He sighed and shook his head. "I'm dead meat."

Mathewson stood up, took a slow step forward, hands in pockets, looking down at Paul.

And for the first time, he saw his mother in him. It was funny, this thing with Paul, because,

Mathewson realized, he'd always somewhat resented the guy, seeing only the father in him. But the mother was there, too.... And just as Elizabeth was a part of him, John Mathewson, brilliant physicist, extraordinary failure as a human being, he knew that so was Paul as well.

And the addition...

The addition enriched him terribly.

"Well," he said. "Not necessarily." And he caught Paul's eyes, and Paul was taken off guard, he knew, because he'd probably never seen stuff like this in Mathewson's eyes before.

"Let's see this thing."

Mathewson reached down and plucked the bomb from Paul's grasp....

No, not plucked, Mathewson realized...

Paul relinquished it. There was no fight. It was as though this were some technical Garden of Gethsemane, and God was plucking the cup from His kid, saying, This is my responsibility! Hell with this crucifixion business!

And Mathewson wheeled about, his hands on the controls of the gadget... wheeled about, showing the thing to the small army assembled with their crown of thorns, their hammers and nails, their spears.

"So!" said Mathewson, a strange triumph flowing through him. "Gentlemen! Fellow sons of bitches! We're all... what we are... right? So, here's my responsible act!"

He glared directly at Lieutenant Colonel Conroy of the United States of America.

"I'm taking him out of here!" said Mathewson.

They all looked like they were looking at a ghost.

"That's right," continued Mathewson, his voice loud and wild. "And since you like scenarios so much, Colonel, I've got one for you! It's kind of a game of chance. I'll bet you... I'll just bet you that I can turn this key, and blow us all to hell, even after you shoot me...." His voice grew stronger, more dramatic, and he could almost feel the fire burning in his eyes. "And you are gonna have to shoot me."

He held the bomb up again, as though to toss it at the assembled brass. They cringed back.

"Okay? Got it? Simple, huh? Everybody's problems solved in a millionth of a second! Now, who wants to play?"

No one, it seemed, cared much for the idea.

"Come on, Paul. Let's go. I've got the feeling that the air out by the lake is a lot fresher than in here."

Paul had already gotten to his feet.

Without question, he went to Mathewson, and the kid's simple trust added measure upon measure to Mathewson's strength.

The SWAT team parted before them, and they walked down the corridor silently, feeling the eyes boring into their backs.

Almost at the reception area, Mathewson broke the silence. "Well," he said. "At least now I can publish."

Paul still seemed a bit numbed by the turn of events. "What do you mean?"

"I mean," said Mathewson, "I think I just lost my security clearance."

"I'm sorry," Paul muttered.

"Hey! No problem! Time to change vocations anyway.... You know what I always wanted to do? Open an ice-cream store in Teaneck, New Jersey."

"I don't know," said Paul. "What kind of ice cream?"

"Plutonium and uranium. Think it will be a hit?"

"I think I've had my share of those flavors, John."

"So have I, Paul," said Mathewson, reaching Security Nest Number One. "So have I."

Chapter Thirty-one

The SWAT troops fell back before them, rank upon rank, like a disciplined army retreating, but ever ready to defend.

It was rather a pathetic sight, thought Lieutenant Colonel Conroy as he stepped into the reception area of MedAtomics and watched Paul Stephens and Dr. John Mathewson step through the front doors. How could you defend against an atomic bomb?

He felt sad.

"Well, we've lost him, all right." He spoke into his portable transceiver. "Red Team, I do not want them off the premises with that gadget. Do you copy?"

"Thank goodness it won't be on the premises," said Wilson.

Joe O'Leary, stationed outside, was watching the two as they went down the front steps. He heard the orders from the colonel and he responded immediately: "Copy, Command. No problem. Gimme a clear shot behind the ear and I'll turn him off like a switch."

O'Leary readied his rifle.

"That's affirmative," said Conroy.

"Yeah, copy. Setting up aim right now."

The swarm of SWATs tensed up, tight as trigger

springs, as Mathewson and Paul continued their walk, bearing their deadly burden.

The metal thing suddenly went *CLICK! BZZZ-ZZZZZZ!*

They could all hear it. The SWAT team, the brass inside over the communications system... and most certainly Mathewson and Paul.

BZZZZZZZ!

And then the sound stopped.

"Uh-oh," said Mathewson.

"What?"

Mathewson pointed at the timer. It was no longer set at 000:02:00. Now it read 999:59:57.

And it was counting down second by second.

Everything seemed frozen.

Except that timer!

"You turned it!" said Paul.

"Nope. Started spontaneously. All by itself. See?" The key was still in first position, unturned.

"Here. I'll fix it!" Paul turned the key to OFF position. But the counter continued to count down. He worked the key back and forth, but to no effect.

Mathewson said, "Neutron flux, probably. Radiation from inside the core can screw up this kind of solid-state time circuit."

"I never heard of that," said Paul.

"Well, live and learn."

Paul was still trying the ON/SET switch, but it didn't work.

Joe O'Leary heard all this. He lowered his rifle and spoke into his tranceiver. "Jesus!"

"What?" demanded Conroy.

"Damn thing's counting down. It's gonna blow!"

State Trooper Steve Henderson heard this on an earphone. No fool he, he threw down his earplug, jumped into his car, and tore off.

"What the hell's with him?" wondered his partner, watching the patrol car speed away.

Colonel Conroy and Lieutenant Morton hurried out the front door, only to be confronted by Dr. Mathewson, holding the bomb.

"Gentlemen," said Mathewson. "We've got a little wrinkle here. Please listen carefully and do exactly what I say."

The timer said 999:95:07.

Dr. John Mathewson laid the bomb down on the laser table gently and looked around at all the electronics and bomb wizards hovering around, wide-eyed, in the room.

Lieutenant Colonel Conroy was right beside them, and all the weapons were gone, forgotten.

"So you're saying," said Conroy, "that we got nine hundred and ninety-nine hours to dismantle it?"

"I don't think so," said Mathewson. "Time base circuits tend to deteriorate exponentially—faster and faster. See?"

It was very obvious: the seconds column was changing very fast, counting down at an ever-increasing rate, the "seconds" ticking off six, seven to the actual second.

"Jesus," said Conroy. "Then why the hell'd we bring it back in here?"

"Why not? Where'd you want to take it?" Mathewson responded, examining the thing very carefully from all angles.

"Anywhere," said Paul, looking on and feeling helpless. "The middle of a large field! Just away from all this plutonium here!"

"A large field? Paul, if this thing goes, you're going to have a really good view of a fifty- to seventy-kiloton explosion!"

Paul's total shock showed on his face. "What? But how?"

"How? Special stuff, Paul," said Mathewson. "Very nasty. It's so hot we don't even know how to test it." He pointed to the small circular plate built into the small sphere. "So—if I unscrew this I can get the core out?"

Paul looked down at the thin groove milled across the diameter to accommodate a screwdriver which allowed it to be screwed into place or removed.

"Okay. Anybody have a screwdriver?" Mathewson asked.

One was thrust in his face.

He took it. "Thanks."

He carefully tried to unscrew the plug. The care brought no results, so he tried force.

"What's wrong?" Conroy demanded impatiently.

"Jammed."

"Give me that," demanded the colonel, taking the screwdriver and straining.

Unsuccessfully.

"You know," said Mathewson, "the same kind of thing happened on the Trinity test, forty years ago— the core stuck halfway in while they were inserting it. . . . I wouldn't push that around too much, by the way."

Conroy looked up. "Why not?"

"You don't want to upset that circuit. It might decide to fire just for spite."

Conroy handed the driver back. "So what do we do?"

"Drill?" asked a bomb expert.

"No time. And you might get a static charge."

Paul looked down, and caught his breath as he saw that the "seconds" column was a blur, and the minutes were ticking off like seconds."

"We could disconnect the batteries!" said Paul.

"Worth a try," said Mathewson.

"I have to remove the middle plate," Paul explained.

"Do it, then," urged Conroy. "Do it."

"I need a Phillips head screwdriver."

Suddenly five Phillips head screwdrivers were thrust toward him. He selected one and started poking about in the guts of the bomb.

A pair of SWAT teamers looked in, weapons dangling, clearly out of their depth and feeling totally useless.

The timer was going absolutely crazy now.

"How much time we got?" asked Conroy.

"I dunno," said Mathewson. "It's an exponential decay."

"Can't you just answer the goddamn question?"

Mathewson took out a small pocket calculator from his breast pocket. He thought for a moment, then looked at Paul.

"Never was good at math.... Paul, as Y approaches infinity, T equals one plus one over n to the—to what?"

"Then the nth, I think," said Paul.

"Very good. Bright kid. You ought to do something with it," Mathewson said breezily.

He punched a few entries into the calculator.

"Okay..." he said. "I make it—about three minutes to zero."

The reaction was not good. Considerable sweat appeared on brows.

"Excuse me, sir," said Morton. "What about evacuating?"

"Evacuation?" said Colonel Conroy. "Evacuation of who?"

"The people—"

"You mean, Pennsylvania, New York, Vermont... Canada...those people?"

"Okay," said Paul. "I've reached the connector."

"Right," said Mathewson. "Go ahead."

"I need a wire cutter."

He inserted the screwdriver a little further.

Suddenly there was a series of ascendingly high-pitched electronic whines. The sound lasted for about five seconds. When it ended, one of the indicator lights on the front panel lit up.

"What's that?" Conroy asked.

"Firing circuit," explained Paul. "The photo-strobes are programmed to charge up at ninety seconds from detonation. I guess the timer's all messed up...." He accepted the wire cutters from somebody, found the wire, and put the blades against red insulation. "Okay. Ready?"

Something was wrong. Mathewson knew it. Something very wrong, and his brain worked furiously to try and figure it out.

"One," said Paul. "Two—"

He increased the pressure on the pliers.

"Omigod! No!" screamed Mathewson. "Wait, wait ...don't cut it! Don't do anything!"

Everyone stared at him with puzzled expressions.

"Don't do anything?" demanded Conroy. "What are you, nuts?"

"Just regular photographic strobe units, that's what you used?" Mathewson asked Paul.

"Uh-huh."

"All right. The problem is, once those things are charged, even if you turn them off, they can discharge while you're unplugging them."

"What's he talking about?" Conroy wanted to know.

"This thing could detonate just from our trying to disconnect it. Okay...now...let me think...just wait."

Conroy was livid. "I'll wait. *It* won't wait!"

"Okay," said Mathewson. "Okay. Either this thing is going to work or it isn't. If it's not going to work, then we can simply sit here and wait for it to reach zero, at which point nothing will happen. However, I happen to think that it is going to work. Which means, we have to disarm it!"

"Yes, but how?" said Conroy.

"Cut the leads from the photo-strobes to the high explosive. How many are there?"

"Six," said Paul.

"Okay. Six leads, six wires. The trick is, we have to cut them all at exactly the same time. And I mean exactly."

"Or what?" said Conroy. And then he got it. "Oh, shit. Really?"

Mathewson's face was grim. "Come on, let's just do it. Cutters."

A bomb specialist in an orange suit pulled a bunch of wire cutters from a toolbox and handed them to Mathewson.

"Where are the leads?" asked Mathewson.

Paul pointed. "This strip here."

"Okay." Mathewson waved at some of the men. "Us three, and you and you and you... come here."

They all huddled around the bomb. Paul looked up and saw that one of them was the guy with DALRYMPLE labeled above his breast pocket. The guy who had tried to shoot him.

"Sorry about before, kid," said Dalrymple through his bushy mustache. "Nothing personal."

The wire cutters were handed around.

Conroy took his and he read off the timer. "Three hundred..."

"Okay," said Mathewson. "Everybody ready?"

"I don't have a cutter," said Paul, holding up empty hands.

"Give me another clipper over here!"

"They're looking," said a bomb technician. "We don't have any more."

Behind them, the technicians were tearing the place apart.

Conroy's face turned absolutely purple. "Are you telling me I'm going to die because some asshole didn't bring a pair of *pliers?*"

Paul's face brightened. "Wait! I got it!"

Jenny's nail clipper! It was still in his pocket, the trusty thing! Ye old Sonic Nail Clipper, better than a Swiss Army knife any day!"

"Two-ten," Conroy reported.

"All right. I'll count backwards from five. Everybody ready?"

"Wait," cried a technician. "Do we cut on one or on zero?"

"One hundred eighty," said Conroy.

"On zero," said Mathewson. "Like this: Three, two, one—this is just a rehearsal, nobody do anything—three, two, one, cut. Everybody understand?"

"One ten," said Conroy.

John smiled grimly. "Okay, anybody wanna make a bet? No? Okay, here we go, for real: Five, four, three, two, one, cut."

That simple.

Clip!

The sound of six clips at once, actually, Mathewson noted with pure scientific objectivity.

But then he thought he was going to faint.

"What do we have?" he said, almost afraid to ask.

Paul looked down at the timer, pretty freaked himself.

The timer said 007:16:45.

And it had stopped.

"We did it!" he cried jubilantly. "We did it."

Amazement and jubilation spread out onto all the faces.

SWAT team members, not knowing what to do with their hands, began shaking each other all around. There was much back patting.

"Well!" said Mathewson, feeling slightly demented. "Everybody awake?"

Then the bomb went off.

Or the photo-strobes, rather, as though the bomb were taking everybody's picture.

Flash! Boom!

Paul jumped, Mathewson jumped, Conroy looked as though he had just suffered a massive seizure.

"Just the photo-strobes!" Mathewson explained.

"Yeah," said Paul.

Like vultures alighting atop a dead thing, the bomb technicians swarmed in to disassemble the bomb.

"Well, say good-bye to it, Paul," said Mathewson, putting a hand on Paul's shoulder.

"Gladly," said Paul. "You know, I never could buy that line in the old thirties movies, about there being things that men should not tamper with. But I'll buy that there are things adolescents shouldn't fool with."

"Hmm? Ah. Well, I think there's a bit of a man somewhere in there, Paul."

"I guess I'm just not the superkid I thought I was."

"You gonna sell your story to the movies?"

"Can I do that from jail?"

"We'll see about that," said Mathewson. "Come on and let's get out of here."

"Are they going to let us?"

"We'll have to see, won't we?"

Together they walked to the large rolling door at the end of the lab. Mathewson reached for a red button above a black button.

Suddenly everything wasn't hunky-dory anymore.

The SWATs tensed up again, and abruptly their guns were in their hands, pointed.

Colonel Conroy called out, "What do you think you two are doing!"

Mathewson hit the button. "Letting a little fresh air in, Colonel!"

The door began to slide up.

"Close that door."

Paul peeked under it, and a thrill raced down his spine.

There they were! They were crawling all over the place, past the state troopers, past the guards! They had come in droves, the people of Ithaca.

They were behind him!

He gazed, astonished, as they gathered at the gate, or walked down the road, or opened the doors of their cars, or parked their bikes.

"Jenny did it!" said Paul.

"Jenny did what?"

"She got the town. They're here! They know!"

The door rolled further up, and Mathewson looked around and smiled at what he saw.

The beat-up old pickup truck that Paul had hotwired pulled up by the gate just that moment.

Jenny got out, and Paul Stephens knew for certain that he had never seen a lovelier sight in his life.

Paul impulsively ran out to the gate and he unlatched it, to let the people—his people, he knew now, not the strangers he'd always thought them—pour in.

"Stop this!" cried Conroy, beside Mathewson now. "You're trespassing on government property!" He seemed particularly troubled by all the cameras evident, all clicking madly.

"Give it up," said Mathewson. "We blew it. What

are you going to do, Conroy? Make everybody disappear? Me, and him, and her—" He pointed to the people, one by one, then made a broad sweeping gesture. "And them?"

A few kids had already walked into the lab and were looking around. "Wow," said one. "Just like in the movies."

"Right," said Mathewson, then he turned to Conroy.

"Too many secrets, Conroy," said Mathewson, feeling a great weight lift from his soul. "Just too many secrets."

"We're moving out," barked Conroy over his headset. "That's right, just necessary security to clear these goddamned kids out!"

Mathewson winked at him, and moved out into the friendly mob.

As the SWAT team and the bomb team and the various other security teams scrambled to obey their master willy-nilly, John Mathewson walked down toward Paul Stephens and Jenny Anderman, reuniting messily.

And there she was, coming toward them all: Elizabeth.

Mathewson joined them, and Jenny impulsively hugged him.

"Paul told me...he told me everything. Thank you," she said, adoration in her eyes.

"John," said Elizabeth. "What...happened?"

"I...I did something," he said, rather astonished at his own words. "For once, I did something, Elizabeth."

"I'll say," said Paul, and he was looking up at Mathewson as though he were some long-lost father.

"I don't understand."

"Later," he said, and he held her close, and then drew in a long breath of fresh fall air.

And he saw the lake, the hills, and the trees alive with the breeze and with their colors. And John Mathewson felt Elizabeth's warmth, and he felt the vibrant aliveness of these people, and the sky and the clouds, and there was, for the first time, no separation, he was a part of it all. Life wasn't just equations and ledger books and atomic numbers anymore.

It was...

Well, it just *was*.

"You know," he said, putting his arm around Paul, "this is really a very pretty place."

"Yeah," said Paul, looking around. He watched the colonel's helicopter rise up like some mammoth dinosaur, dip, and soar away, making the most awful sound. "And it's getting prettier by the moment."

They walked through the gate, toward the waiting news reporters.